THE GHOST LAKE CHRONICLES

BOOK 1 THE LEGEND

FRANK D. ANSELMO

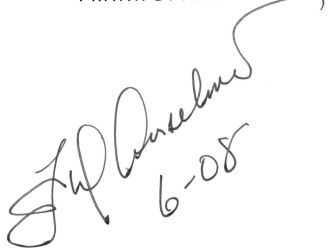

6-08

Cover design by:
Branden Apitz
Aluna Group Inc.
bapitz@alunadesign.com

ISBN: 1-4196-9289-5
ISBN-13: 9781419692895

Visit www.booksurge.com to order additional copies.

This book is dedicated to my wife, Noreen,
my seven children, John, Greg, Anne, Shelly, Gino,
Aimee, and Carissa and to my sixteen grandchildren.
May the importance of family be instilled in
them forever.

THE GHOST LAKE CHRONICLES

TABLE OF CONTENTS

NEW FRIENDS

✤ ✤ ✤

Sunlight slowly crept across my pillow, stirring me from a deep sleep. Opening my eyes, I yawned and smiled at the thought of a new day and wondered what it had in store for me. The last week had brought me more excitement than I ever could have imagined and it had been an adventure that most kids my age could only dream about.

Most of my summer had been fairly boring up to this point and I was looking forward to school starting in a couple of weeks. My friends lived across town and I didn't get to see many of them except on the fourth of July when the whole town got together on Main Street for the big celebration. This year the celebration was bigger than usual. It was 1952 and Ghost Lake Minnesota was celebrating its 80Th anniversary. There had been a big parade in the morning with two marching bands and about ten different floats from the different stores in town. The parade was followed by kid's races and contests of different kinds. I took third place in the sack race and teamed up with Henry Johnson to take second in the three legged race. We each put a leg in the same sack and arms around each others shoulders, then stumbled, jumped and ran the hundred yards across the football field, only falling twice, but that was over a month ago and summer had become a series of hot days with not much to do. My dad has been working every day and I'd been staying close to home helping mom and running errands.

I lived for the weekends when the movie theater came up with a new matinee movie for kids. Last weekend it was JIM BRIDGER-MOUNTAIN MAN. Mom gave me a quarter for the movie and I had more than enough money. The movie cost twelve cents, leaving me with thirteen cents to spend on treats. I bought a nickel ice cream cone, a nickel bag of popcorn, and a little bag of candy which I could get three pieces for a penny. Into the dimly lit theater I went with my hands full of goodies and found a few of my school friends down near the front and we settled down to watch the latest adventure. All of us cheered near the end when Jim Bridger came down from the mountains to save a frontier settlement from an Indian attack.

I went home with my head spinning with dreams of Jim Bridger and of exploring unknown territory and establishing a fort on some wild frontier. It wasn't until Monday that I came up with the idea of crossing Ghost Lake Road and exploring the woods beyond. It was only two blocks from my house, but it was an area that I had never explored. The first time I went exploring I took my dad's compass and took a reading before I went into the woods. The compass told me I was going in South, so I knew I would have to come back North to get to the road. It was a trick that my

Dad had taught me when he took me hunting last fall. I actually didn't go in very far as I wasn't sure what I was going to find. I had only gone in about a hundred yards, gradually going up a slight rise to the top of a flat topped hill. I followed the edge of the hill and discovered a clump of birch trees. I immediately knew that these trees would be perfect for a tree fort. I could nail rungs up on two of the trees and when I reached the right height I could nail cross bars to three of the trees and put a platform across. I could then put railings around it so I could stand up without falling out of it. As I walked out of the woods I was mentally figuring what tools I would need to bring the next day to complete the project.

The next morning found me back at the birch clump with a hatchet, hammer, nails, and a small bow saw. By midmorning I had cut down enough small saplings for the rungs and three larger ones for the platform braces. At noon I finished nailing the rungs and found myself about fifteen feet off the ground. After a short break, I brought the larger pieces up one at a time and nailed them in place to make the base of the platform. This was enough for one day. I hid the tools behind a bush and mentally made plans for the next day.

That evening I found some scrap boards in the garage and decided they would make the perfect floor for my tree fort. I tied them in a bundle and carried them on my back into the woods the next morning. Within an hour my tree fort had a floor, but I was still unsure about standing up on it without railings. Another trip down the rungs and into the surrounding woods brought me to some small saplings that were the perfect size for my railings. In a short time they were cut, hauled, carried up and nailed in place.

I then stood up and tested it out. Holding on to the railing I looked all around and nodded my head in satisfaction. This was going to be all right!

From my lofty perch I could just about see Ghost Lake Road, down the hill from me. As I turned around on the platform, I noticed that one of the railings was a little wobbly. I picked up the hammer and went to work. I had just finished pounding in the second nail when out of the corner of my eye I caught some movement down below me and to my left. My first thought was that it must be Arnold Barnswell, my mortal enemy, sneaking up on me to pull some kind of dirty trick. Arnold and I had not gotten along since kindergarten when he filled my gym shoes with sand from the sandbox.

Watching closely, I saw him sneak behind a little evergreen tree. I was not about to let Arnold think he was getting the best of me, so I stood up and shouted down at him. "I see you Arnold, behind that little tree, so you might as well come out." Arnold crawled out from behind the little tree and stood up, only to my surprise, it wasn't Arnold, but some strange kid I had never seen before.

Hanging on to my handrail, I leaned over and peered down at the stranger. He walked over to the base of my tree with his head leaned back and his hand cupped over his eyes to shade the sun. He was about my age, a little taller than me, with short, bright red hair and freckles. I was sure I had never seen him before.

"Hi!" I called down. "Who are you? Where did you come from?"

The boy grinned up at me and rubbed his crew cut hair. "Hi! I'm Scooter Dobson...I just moved to town two days ago. I was just walking down that road down there and I heard you pounding. That's a nice looking tree fort you've got."

"Thanks." I called back. "C'mon up. There's room for both of us."

Scooter slowly pulled himself up the rickety rungs I had nailed to the birch tree. Poking his head up over the edge of the platform, he looked at me with raised eyebrows. "Are you sure this thing will hold the both of us?"

"Yeah, I'm sure." I said confidently, "I used big spikes and good solid wood."

Thrusting his leg up over the side, Scooter managed to squirm up onto the platform. He crawled over to the handrail, cautiously pulled himself up and peeked over the edge. Grabbing a handful of leaves from a nearby branch, he tore them off and let them flutter down to the ground. "Woweee......," he half-whispered, "That's a long way down."

"It is, isn't it?" I said, peering over the handrail. "I guess I got a little carried away." Turning to Scooter, I offered my hand. "I'm Randy...Randy Bigsley."

Scooter shook my hand vigorously. "Hi Randy, I'm glad to meet you! What's your real name?"

"Randall," I answered, "But nobody calls me that. My uncle started calling me Randy when I was a little kid and everyone has been calling me that ever since."

"I know what you mean. My real name is Leonard, but nobody ever calls me anything but Scooter."

There was a moment of awkward silence as I had not had much practice in meeting new kids. Since we had nothing in common, I figured the next best thing was to ask him about himself. "So, Scooter," I began, "How old are you? What grade are you in? Where do you live?"

"Whoa! Whoa!" Scooter said holding up his hand. "One question at a time."

"O.K., I'm sorry." I said sheepishly, "How old are you?"

"I'll be twelve on the thirty first of October."

"Hey! Halloween!" I exclaimed. "That's pretty neat."

"How about you Randy, how old are you?"

"I'll be twelve in December. What grade are you in?"

"Sixth." Scooter answered. "How about you?"

"That's great! I'll be in sixth too. We'll be in the same class because we only have one of each grade in this town."

"Do you know who our teacher will be?" Scooter asked.

"Miss Williams." I answered. "You'll like her, she's nice."

"Why did you call me Arnold before?" Scooter asked.

"Oh, when I saw you sneaking around down there, I thought for sure it was this kid, Arnold Barnswell. He's a jerk from our class that's always bugging me."

"Why is he a jerk?" Scooter asked.

"I don't know...he just is. He's the kind of kid who always thinks he's cool and is mean to other kids. I've never seen him be nice or do anything kind for anybody.

"What did you think he was doing here?"

"Oh, he'd probably wait until I was gone and then come back and wreck my tree fort and then brag about it to his friends."

"Boy, he does sound like a jerk!"

Scooter and I continued to question each other. I learned that he had moved into a house only about a block away from me and like me was an only child. We hit it off great and I knew that Scooter was going to be a good friend. It was going to be great starting off the school year having a head start on knowing the new kid in class. After sitting in the tree fort and talking for about an hour, we finally climbed down and headed down the path to Ghost Lake Road.

"What're you doing tomorrow, Randy?" Scooter asked as we came out on the road.

"I don't know for sure...I'll probably come back up here to the tree fort. I want to chop away some of the brush from around the tree."

"Great!" said Scooter, "Do you mind if I join you? I can bring a hatchet and a machete."

"A machete?" I asked, "What's a machete?"

"It's a big, long, wide, knife-like sword that natives in the jungles use for cutting brush and chopping off the heads of their enemies."

I wasn't sure what Scooter was describing, but it sure sounded like a terrible weapon and I was most curious to see it. "Yeah, sure." I answered. "I can use the help. Let's bring some sandwiches and lemonade and make a day of it."

"Good idea!" exclaimed Scooter as we walked along. "Where shall we meet, and at what time?

"How about right here where the path goes in...About ten o'clock."

"That sounds good to me." Scooter said as he turned off to go to his house. "See you tomorrow at ten."

"See you, Scooter." I said watching him go off. This was going to be interesting. I finally felt like I had met a friend that I could tell private things to and could trust. I don't know why, but in that short time, I had sensed that Scooter was going to be a special friend to me.

THE CAMPSITE

❈ ❈ ❈

The hazy morning sun was just beginning to climb above the trees as I sat on the edge of Ghost Lake Road, waiting for Scooter to show up. I was watching a colony of ants as they scurried back and forth from their ant hill at the road's edge to a tiny little tunnel in the grass that grew along the ditch. They would enter the grass empty handed and emerge with some kind of material to carry back to their hill. I was trying to imagine what it must be like to be as small as they were and what the world must look like to them. I had become so emerged in my fantasy world that I didn't hear Scooter as he rode up on his bike.

"Hey Randy!" he exclaimed. "What are you doing down in the ditch?"

I nearly jumped out my skin. "Gee Scooter!" I scolded, "Do you have to sneak up on a guy like that? You almost gave me a heart attack."

"I'm sorry." he apologized. "I wasn't trying to scare you. What are you doing down there?"

"I'm watching ants." I replied.

"Watching ants? What do you mean, watching ants?"

Scooter had obviously grown up in a city and had never watched ants. "I mean I'm watching ants." I said with some impatience. "Haven't you ever watched ants?"

"No. I can't say that I ever have. What do you watch for?"

That was a good question. One I had never thought of. "Uh...I don't know...I just watch. I see what they're carrying and where they're going with it, and sometimes they have a fight over something...all kinds of neat stuff like that."

"No kidding!" Scooter exclaimed. "That sounds like fun. Are we still going to clear the underbrush around your tree fort?"

"Our tree fort." I corrected. "Since you know where it is and are now my best friend, it's your tree fort also."

"It is? Gee, thanks!" Scooter exclaimed. "So, let's go cut some brush."

"Did you bring your machete?" I asked.

"Did I bring the machete?" Scooter said with a grin. "Does a beaver have teeth?" Scooter dug in his pack sack and brought forth a long, sharp, broad-bladed machete.

"Wow!" I exclaimed. "That does look like it could lop off a head."

"Slick as a whistle." Scooter said as he raised the machete over his head and brought it down with a resounding thunk on a dead log in the ditch. "Yup," He grunted as he pried the blade out of the log. "Slick as a whistle."

"I'm impressed." I said with awe. "Yuk! Can you imagine what that thing would do to soft flesh?"

We made our way up the hill and arrived at the base of our tree fort. Setting our tools down, we walked around, trying to determine a good place to start. Since our tree fort was right on the brink of the hill, we decided to begin there and work our way back toward a more level area.

"Why don't we take turns?" Scooter asked, "I'll chop brush for a while and you can haul it away. Then we'll switch and you can chop for a while."

"Sounds good to me." I answered. Actually, I preferred that Scooter chop first, so I could observe how he used the machete. I didn't want to seem like a rookie when I began.

Scooter took the machete and began hacking away at the brush around the base of the tree. I could see where the machete was the right tool for the job, as it only took one or two swings to cut the small saplings down. In a short time Scooter had cut a small pile of brush and I dragged it away and piled it at the side of the hill.

In about fifteen minutes Scooter turned to me, wiping his brow, "Want to take a turn at it, Randy?"

We traded places and I got my chance to swing the machete. It wasn't as difficult as I thought, and in a short time I had gotten the hang of it and was cutting brush like an old-timer. As I looked around, I saw that we already had made a sizable clearing from the tree fort back to a level area where the hill leveled off. Here the brush thinned out and the cutting went much faster.

"Let's take a break." I said as I cut down the last few saplings in the clearing.

"Sounds good to me!" Scooter exclaimed. "Is it time for lunch yet?"

"Not yet." I said, looking at my watch. "But let's have a glass of lemonade and a snack anyway."

Scooter dug in his pack sack and brought out a fruit jar of lemonade. "Rats!" he exclaimed, "I forgot to bring glasses."

"No big deal." I said. "We can drink right from the jar. Here, have a peanut butter sandwich."

"Thanks." Scooter said, handing me the jar for the first drink.

I sat down with my back against a birch tree, unscrewed the jar and took a long swig of lemonade. "Ahhhh....that hits the spot." I passed the jar over to Scooter and looked around at the work we had just completed. "This is really looking good Scooter."

"It sure is." Scooter commented. "It almost reminds me of one of those campsites you see at the state parks."

Campsite! The idea struck us both at the same time like a thunderbolt from the sky. We turned and looked at each other with open mouths, each knowing what the other was thinking.

"Are you thinking what I'm thinking?" Scooter asked.

"Do you have a tent?" I asked hopefully.

"Do I have a tent?" Scooter questioned. "Does a bear sleep in the woods?"

"Really? What kind is it?"

"It's an old army surplus pup tent that my uncle gave me. It's kind of old, but it's better than nothing."

"That's all right." I assured him. "We want to rough it anyway. Do you think we could both fit in it?"

"I'm sure." Scooter said with certainty. "It's only going to be for one night anyway."

"Well then, let's make some plans!"

Scooter stood up and began walking around the clearing. "We should probably come back here with a rake and shovel and make a nice level spot for the tent."

"And a fire-pit!" I added. "We can't have a campsite without a fire-pit."

"Good idea! I think the tent should go over here. It's kind of level and if we put the fire-pit in the center of the clearing, it'll be far enough away in case of sparks and smoke."

"Yeah, and we can gather some firewood this afternoon and by the way, when should we plan on camping?"

"The sooner the better, maybe even tonight if we can get all the arrangements made."

Then Scooter came up with the inevitable question. It was a question which both of us had been thinking about and worrying about. "Do you think our parents will let us camp out away from home?"

"I don't know Scoot; they've let me camp out before, but only in the back yard. But then I was little and now that I'm going into the sixth grade I don't see what the big deal is. They're going to have to cut the apron strings sooner or later. It's not like we're going two hundred miles away for two weeks or anything like that."

"Well," Scooter said, "If your mom can be convinced, I'm sure mine can be. Your mom could call my mom and talk to her. With her being new in town, I think she would listen to someone's mom who's been here for a long time."

"Is your mom a worrier?" I asked.

"Is my mom a worrier?" Scooter answered. "Does a dog bark?"

"I know what you mean." I commented. "My mom would worry if she heard of a criminal escaping in Russia."

"Do you think your mom will call my mom?" Scooter asked.

"I think so, but first we have to convince her."

Scooter got up and picked up his machete and pack sack. "Well, let's go ask her. We'll never know if we don't ask."

Visions of camping raced through our minds as we made our way out of the woods and down to the road. Scooter was the first to think of a new dimension. "Hey! I've got a great idea! I'll bring my dog Blanca! She's a German Shepherd Husky mix and I guarantee we wouldn't have to be afraid of nothing if she was with us!"

"Super!" I said excitedly. "And that will probably help convince our moms too!"

"Boy! This is going to be great!" Scooter exclaimed as we stepped out of the woods and onto Ghost Lake Road.

No sooner had we gotten on the road, when we saw Arnold riding up on his bike. I didn't even get a chance to warn Scooter that this was Arnold, the creep I had been telling him about.

Arnold came to skidding halt on the loose gravel, showering us with small stones and sand. He looked at Scooter, put out his hand like Floyd Smooth and said, "Hi kid! Arnold Barnswell. What's your name?"

"Scooter Dobson." Scooter answered, shaking Arnold's hand.

"So, what are you guys up to?" Arnold questioned, studying our machete and hatchet. "Planning on murdering somebody?"

Yeah, you Arnold! I thought to myself. This guy thought he was so cool, it was sickening. I just couldn't bring myself to be civil to him.

Scooter, on the other hand, being the nice kid that he was, and not really knowing Arnold, laughed at Arnold's remark and answered. "No, we're going to camp out in the woods here tonight."

I couldn't believe it! He had done it! Scooter had actually given out the most secret of information to my most mortal enemy! If only I could have warned him ahead of time.

Arnold quickly slipped into his true form. "Ha!" He sneered. "You guys will never make it through the night. If you hear an owl hoot or a frog croak, you girls will take off for home."

"You forget one thing, Arnold." I quickly jumped in. "We're not born sissies like you."

"Oh yeah?" Arnold said, bringing forth from his pocket a brand new shiny jack-knife. "I'll bet this brand new jack-knife against that machete that you won't make it through the night."

"C'mon Arnold." I laughed. "That machete is worth five jack-knives, and besides I don't want to bet."

"Yeah, and I know why. You're chicken!"

That was too much for Scooter. He was not about to let Arnold stand there and call us chickens. "Wait a minute, Arnold, before you start calling anyone chicken. In the first place, this machete is my dad's and not mine to be betting on. In the second place, if you want to bet, let's bet on something that won't cost anyone anything."

"Like what?" Arnold said suspiciously.

"Let me think a minute." Scooter said, pausing to rub his nose. "How about if whoever loses has to run down Main Street in his underwear."

"Get out! What are you...crazy or what?" Arnold exclaimed.

"What's the matter Arnold?" Scooter teased. "Are you chicken?"

"No, but I'm not crazy either. I'll tell you what. I'll bet you twenty-five used comic books that you won't make it through the night."

"You're on!" We both exclaimed. I wanted to add that the bet was on only if we could get permission from our mom's, but that wouldn't have appeared very manly. Besides, I had tons of old comics in case I lost.

"O.K. tough guys. I'll meet you here at seven tomorrow morning and you better be able to prove that you stayed in the woods all night!"

"We'll see you at seven!" I exclaimed. "C'mon Scooter, let's go."

"Yeah," said Scooter, "We'll see you at seven, and Arnold, why don't you bring the comics with you so we don't have to keep hounding you for them."

I wondered if we had bitten off more than we could chew as I turned to see Arnold watching us go up the road. Getting our mom's permission was going to be our first obstacle, and then if we did, we still had to stay overnight in the woods and I knew down deep that the woods were going to be a lot different in the darkness of night.

THE LEGEND

❖ ❖ ❖

"Let me do the talking, Scooter." I said as we approached the back door of my house. "I think I can sweet talk her into letting us camp out."

"O.K." Scooter said, "But I don't even know your mom and she might think I'm weird or something."

"Nah..." I assured him, "I've already told her you're a nice kid, and all you have to do is to remember to say please and thank you and all that stuff."

"Wait a minute." Scooter said, stopping and twisting his ear.

"What are you doing?" I said with amused curiosity.

"I'm turning on my charm!" Scooter said with a grin. "O.K., I'm ready, bring on your mom!"

I held back a giggle while opening the door, showing Scooter into our back porch. "Hi Mom! I'm home." I called as we entered the kitchen.

Scooter stood quietly by the door with a half-smile, waiting to be introduced.

Mom entered the kitchen with a smile. "Hi boys! Come on in."

"Mom..." I began, "This is Scooter Dobson, the new boy I told you about."

Mom extended her hand in greeting. "How do you do Scooter, Randy has told me a lot about you."

"How do you do ma'am." Scooter said with warm feeling. "I'm pleased to meet you, and I must say that you are much younger and prettier than I had imagined."

Wow! I thought to myself. This kid can really lay on the charm!

Mom blushed. "Well, thank you Scooter. That is one of the nicest compliments that I've ever had!"

"You're welcome ma'am." Scooter answered politely.

I figured there was no time like the present, so I interrupted the small talk with the big question. "Uh, mom?" Scooter and I have this great idea! "We'd like to camp out tonight...What do you think?"

Mom wrinkled her nose and raised her eyebrows, thinking for a few moments...I don't know Randy...you don't have a tent and the weatherman said there is a possibility of showers tonight."

"Not to worry Mom! Scooter's got a tent and if it did rain a little, it wouldn't hurt us. C'mon mom, I'm almost twelve and not a little kid anymore, please!"

"I don't know." Mom said weakening. "Why don't we wait and ask your dad when he gets home from work."

"O.K. mom, Scooter and I have to finish fixing up the camp site anyway, and then we have to get our gear together. We can do all that while we're waiting for dad."

"Camp site?" Mom asked wide-eyed. "What do you mean, camp site and where is this?"

"It's by my tree fort, in the woods by Ghost Lake Road. It's right on the edge of town mom."

"Oh no, Randy!" She said sternly, "I won't have you camping by any lake. I wouldn't sleep a wink all night. Besides, I heard that years ago a boy about your age wandered in those woods and was never seen again."

"Who was that?" I asked.

"I don't know. I remember Grandpa Johnson talking about it one time."

"But mom," I argued, "It's nowhere near the lake, honest. It's right near the road. We could probably see the street lights from our camp site."

"And I'm going to bring my dog!" Scooter chimed in. "She's a Husky-Shepherd mix and an excellent watch dog. She wouldn't let any harm come to us."

"Oh, I don't know." Mom said weakening again. "I'll talk to your father when he comes home and we'll see what he says."

That sounded good to me. I knew dad would be on our side, as I remembered him telling me about when he used to go camping when he was a kid. Dads had a way of understanding boys better than moms.

"What does Scooter's mother think of this camping trip?" Mom asked.

"I don't know, ma'am." Scooter answered. "We haven't told her about it yet."

"Well, I think you had better talk to her first, before you make any more plans."

In a short time Scooter and I arrived at his house. Scooter introduced me to his mom and she was really nice, in fact, she reminded me of my mom a lot. She was a little easier to convince on the camping question, as she was new in town and decided to rely on my parent's judgment. She took my phone number and said she would call my mom and talk to her about it. We decided that to let it go at that and head back to the camp site for our final preparations.

"Let's go back to my house and pick up a rake and shovel so we can level an area for the tent and dig a fire pit." I suggested.

"Good idea!" Scooter agreed.

We picked up the rake and shovel and headed down Ghost Lake Road, full of ideas of the camp out.

About two hundred yards down Ghost Lake Road, we passed by Grandpa Johnson's house. Grandpa Johnson was one of the oldest friends of our family. Everyone in town called him Grandpa Johnson, or Gramps, but as far as I knew he didn't have any relatives. I guess he had been a bachelor all his life. My mom always liked him and had him over to our house for special occasions like Thanksgiving and Christmas. I kind of felt sorry for him, living all alone for all those years.

Gramps was working out in his garden as we passed by and he called out to us. "Hello Randy! Who's your new partner?"

"Hi Gramps!" I called back. "This is Scooter Dobson, he just moved to town this week."

"Is that your Grandpa?" Scooter whispered.

"No...Shhhh! I'll explain later. C'mon, let's go over and I'll introduce you."

As we approached Gramp's garden fence, Gramps put down his hoe and came to greet us. Reaching over the fence, he put his hand out to Scooter. "Glad to meet you, son, you can just call me Gramps."

Scooter shook his hand. "Glad to meet you, sir."

Gramps noticed our rake and shovel and asked. "What are you two boys up to with a rake and shovel?"

I didn't mind telling Gramps about our plans as I knew he'd understand about boys wanting to go camping. "We're fixing up a campsite in the woods across the road a ways and we're planning on camping out there tonight."

Gramps raised his bushy, white, eyebrows and asked. "You boys aren't scared of camping out alone?"

"No sir! "I answered. "Why, should we be?"

"Well, no." Gramps stammered. "I just thought that with the legend and all."

Legend? Scooter and I looked at each other with wonder. "What legend are you talking about Gramps?" I asked.

"Why...its how the Town of Ghost Lake got its name. You mean to tell me that nobody ever told you about the legend of the lost boy of Ghost Lake?"

"No. I can't say that I've ever heard about it...Wait! My mom said something today about some kid that was supposed to have wandered off years ago and was never found, but she never said anything about a legend or a ghost."

Scooter chimed in excitedly. "Well, I just moved to town this week and I haven't heard anything about anything! I'd like to know about the legend. What is it?"

I looked closely at Gramps. I wasn't sure if he was pulling our leg or not, but I was dying to hear more. This could be like a real mystery that I had dreamed about for years. "Is this for real?" I questioned.

"Well, that's how the town got its name, and it was even written up in a newspaper article one time. Some reporter was writing on the history of the town and told the whole story of the legend."

Scooter was losing patience. "C'mon Gramps, tell us the whole story."

"You have to realize," Gramps began, "In the early part of the century, this town was not much more than a crude settlement with just a few scattered houses, a post office, and a store or two. Most of the surrounding country-side was heavily forested and there were very few roads."

"Were there a lot of wild animals?" Scooter asked.

"Oh yes. There were deer, wolves, bear and moose all around here at that time."

"What about the boy?" I asked, getting back to the subject.

"Well, he was a boy about your age and it was about this time of the year, when the berries are ripe, that he disappeared."

"Disappeared?" Scooter gulped.

"Yep...vanished from the face of the earth."

"How?" I asked.

"Nobody knows. It seems he left home one day to go picking blueberries in the woods over here." At this point Gramps pointed in the general direction of where our camp site was. "It was somewhere between here and the west bay of Ghost Lake. Anyway, he never came home. The next day his folks and a bunch of people from the settlement formed a search party and searched the woods. In fact, they searched for several days, but never turned up a trace of the lost boy. The only thing they found was one of the berry pails that the boy was using, but that's all. They even dragged the lake but found nothing. This went on for a week or so and then they finally gave up. They never did find him or even a clue of what might have happened."

"What did his parents do after that?" Scooter asked.

"I guess they stuck around until the next spring and then moved on. I reckon they were kind of drifters anyway."

"What do you think happened to him, Gramps?" I asked.

"I haven't the foggiest notion." Gramps said, scratching his head. "But, there have been plenty of theories around town down through the years."

"Like what?" Scooter asked.

"Oh, some folks say that a bear or wolf got him, and then some say that maybe he wandered clear out of the country or maybe drowned in the lake and was never found. "There were lots of different ideas, but no proof of any of them. I can't say that I believe any of them."

"Why not Gramps?" I asked.

"Because, whatever happened to him, there should have been some clue or something...I just don't know."

"Is that the legend, then?" Scooter asked curiously.

"No, that was only part of the mystery. The rest came later on that summer and then again a few years later."

Gramps had us eating out of his hand now. This was becoming the mystery I had been hoping for. "What do you mean, only part of the mystery?" I whispered.

"Well, later that summer, a couple of fishermen were over in the west bay of Ghost Lake. It was toward evening and they were fishing just a way out from shore, when they saw a young boy come out of the woods and down to the lakeshore. He ran along the beach a ways and when they hollered to him, he turned and ran back into the woods."

"What's so strange about that?" Scooter asked.

"Like I said, this was almost wilderness back then and nobody lived anywhere near there. Anyway, when they came in from fishing they were telling someone at a local tavern about what they had seen and their description fit the lost boy perfectly."

"You're kidding!" I exclaimed.

"No. They even said he was carrying a berry pail."

Scooter and I looked at each other with wide eyes. "Is there any more?" Scooter croaked.

"Yes there was another incident a few years later. An old woman was walking down this very road one evening and she claimed she heard a voice in the woods crying and calling for help."

"Who was it?" I asked, not sure if I really wanted to know.

"Nobody, as far as anyone could tell." Gramps said with a puzzled look.

"Uhh ...by the way," Scooter asked hesitatingly, "Is that how Ghost Lake got its name

"Yup." Gramps said, "They figured that what those two fishermen saw and what the old woman heard, was the ghost of the lost boy, so they began calling it Ghost Lake and this little town that grew out of the settlement be-came Ghost Lake also."

"Have there been any other weird things happen since that time?" I asked.

"Not really anything anyone could put their finger on." Gramps pondered, then went on. "But, from time to time, people who live along the road here claim that sometimes in the dead of night their dogs act strange and growl and bark at what appears to be nothing. But then, dogs are always barking at skunks and coons. Although some people say that animals have a sixth sense and can sense things that people can't."

"Like ghosts?" Scooter asked, his voice breaking as he looked at me. I didn't know what to think. I enjoyed a mystery, but I wasn't sure if I'd enjoy an encounter with a ghost.

"Maybe," Gramps said, "But I don't hold with any spirits or ghosts. I've enough trouble with the real world."

I couldn't help it. I had to ask Gramps the question, at the risk of offending him. "Gramps," I began. "I don't mean to be rude or say I don't believe you, but you wouldn't happen to be telling us a tall tale to scare us... would you?

Gramps chuckled, "No, I know it sounds like a strange story, but you can go to the public library and look it up in the newspaper. They'll have a copy of the write-up about the history of Ghost Lake. Just ask Mrs. Randall, the librarian, she'll help you find it."

I looked at Scooter. He was probably thinking the same thing I was thinking. "Well Gramps," I said, "We've got to go and get our camp site ready. Thanks for telling us the story of the legend."

Scooter took the hint. "Yeah, we'd better get going. Thanks Gramps. It's been nice meeting you and visiting you."

"Yes, stop by anytime." Gramps invited. "I hope I didn't scare you with that story. I'm sure you'll be perfectly safe camping over in the woods, and if you need any help during the night, I'll be right here."

"O.K. thanks Gramps." we chorused as we waved and walked back out on Ghost Lake Road.

Neither of us spoke for a full minute as we walked down the road toward our camp site. Finally I broke the silence. "What do you think, Scooter? Shall we finish the camp site or go to the library?"

Scooter looked at his watch. "Well, it's only a little after one, we could go to the library and still have time to finish the camp site."

"Let's go then! I'm dying to find out if what Gramps told us is true, and if it is...Oh well, let's find out first and worry about the ghost later. C'mon, we can hide the rake and shovel in the woods over here and pick them up on our way back."

"Good idea!" Scooter exclaimed, "Let's go!"

UNCLE HENRY

✤ ✤ ✤

Going up the library steps, Scooter turned to me and asked. "Say Randy, if we find out that Gramps' story is true, are we still going to camp out?"

I had thought about that and I had to admit it did present a problem and the problem had only one solution. "Well, I don't really see where we have any choice after our little bet with Arnold." That was rotten luck on our part. If only we had talked to Gramps before we made the bet with Arnold, we would have had a choice as to whether we would camp out or not, and then there was the fact that we really hadn't gotten permission yet.

"How bad do you want to win the bet with Arnold?" Scooter asked.

"I'll tell you what Scooter, there's no way I'm going to let Arnold win! I don't care if there's a ghost in my sleeping bag, I'm staying all night!"

"All right!" Scooter exclaimed as he opened the door of the library.

We stepped into the dim gloom of the old library and detected an odor of old varnish and musty books. Apparently this was a slow time of the day, as we were all alone except for Mrs. Randall, the librarian.

Scooter turned to me and whispered. "It's spooky in here. Maybe it's best that we don't find anything on the legend. I mean, what we don't know, won't hurt us."

"I thought of that." I whispered back, "But then again, maybe the story isn't as bad as it sounds either."

"Well," Scooter said, "If we find out anything really scary, we'll just stop reading."

I smiled and nodded as we walked up to Mrs. Randall's desk. "Hello Mrs. Randall, we're looking for an article about how Ghost Lake got its name, and we're wondering if you could help us."

"Hello boys. Yes, I can help you. It seems that those articles are very popular today. Just this morning a man was in doing research on a similar subject."

"Does he live here in town, ma'am?" I asked, thinking that maybe it was Gramps.

"No he doesn't." she answered, "And that's the strange part about it. He said he was looking up his family history and lived here many years ago. He claims that the lost boy of Ghost Lake was his older brother. Can you imagine that?"

I felt a shiver go up my spine. This was turning into more of a mystery than I could have imagined. "His brother?" I asked.

"Yes, and he said that he would offer a reward of a hundred dollars to anyone providing information which would help in finding out what happened to his lost brother."

Scooter turned to me with a grin. I could see the wheels turning in his head. "Thank you Mrs. Randall." I said as she handed me a large folder containing the old newspapers.

Scooter nudged me in the ribs as we made our way over to a table by the window. "A hundred bucks!" he whispered. "Wouldn't that be something?"

"It sure would." I said, digging out the pile of papers. "Here, you go through this pile and I'll take these."

The first few articles told of the beginning of Ghost Lake and how the settlement grew from a small group of homesteaders into the community it is today. It was interesting, but not what we were looking for. I skipped ahead a few years and there it was!

"Bingo!" I whispered, "Here it is, Scooter!"

"Wow!" He whispered as he stared at the headline. LOST BOY HAUNTS NEARBY WOODS

We both hunched over and skimmed through the article. It was pretty much like what Gramps had told us, with a few more details. Included was a map of the area that the boy was lost in, showing where the search party had covered. I shuddered as I noted that our camp site was approximately in the center of the map. This was really getting freaky!

"Listen!" Scooter said as he read from the article. "John Frankson, age 13, was never seen or heard from again. Authorities are assuming that the boy is dead and that his remains are still in the area in which he was lost."

"What year was that?" I questioned.

"Let's see," Scooter said, skimming back to the beginning of the article. "It was August 20, 1892... That's exactly sixty years ago."

"Would a ghost stick around for that many years?" I asked.

"Heck yes!" Scooter exclaimed. "Did you ever read about those ghosts in those English castles? Some of them have been haunting those old places for hundreds of years. Besides, what's a year to a ghost?"

"I guess I never thought of it that way." I said, wishing I hadn't asked the question.

We continued reading the article and found more facts that we hadn't know about. "Look here Scooter! It says that the boy's father reported an old Colt revolver missing and it was assumed that the boy had taken it with him."

"Why would he take a gun with him?" Scooter asked.

"Remember what Gramps said, that there were lots of wild animals around back then, like wolves and bears? I would have taken a gun too."

"Is there anything else?" Scooter said as I looked up and slowly closed the folder.

"No, it's pretty much like Gramps told us, except for the gun and the date."

"Wow!" Scooter exclaimed. "Can you imagine? We're going to be camping in the same woods that the lost boy's ghost is haunting?"

"Shut up Scooter! I don't even want to think about it. Besides, it's not for sure. Nobody ever saw the ghost or has any proof that it exists."

"What about those fishermen?" Scooter argued.

"They said they saw a boy, not a ghost."

"Well, I still think it was a ghost and not the boy."

"Let's get out of here." I said standing up. "This place gives me the creeps."

We returned the article to Mrs. Randall and stepped out into the bright sunshine and fresh air. "Well Randy."

Scooter asked as we walked slowly down the steps. "What now?"

I thought for a moment before answering. "We still go. I've never heard of a ghost ever killing anyone, or even hurting anyone for that matter, so what do we have to be afraid of?"

"That's right!" Scooter said bravely. "And besides, we'll have Blanca with us. She'll rip that ghost's sheet to shreds!"

We both laughed to relieve the tension as we walked down the street. "What shall we do first?" I asked.

"Let's see," Scooter said, stopping and looking at his watch. "It's almost three o'clock. We could go to my house, pick up the tent and Blanca, grab a few clothes and groceries and not have to come back later."

It was amazing! Scooter had a gift for organizing. I didn't have the faintest idea where to begin, but Scooter seemed to see everything in the order that it should happen. I would have probably forgotten the tent or the poles or something.

"O.K." Scooter said, counting on his fingers as we walked up the sidewalk. "We'll need the basic things for survival in the wilderness, food, water, or a more suitable substance like soda pop. Shelter, which in this case happens to be my World War II army surplus pup tent, and last but not least, something to keep us entertained. "Do you have any ideas?"

"I've got stacks of comic books. We could take a pile of them and we can read in the tent by flashlight."

"Great! And how about playing cards? There's nothing like a game of war to pass the time away."

"Cards it is!" I exclaimed as we walked up the sidewalk to Scooter's house.

"Mom, I'm home!" Scooter called as we entered the kitchen. No answer. "Mom? Anybody home?" No answer. "What the heck is going on?" Scooter mumbled as we walked into the living room and then back to the kitchen.

"Maybe she had to go out for a while." I suggested.

"Yeah, here's a note." Scooter said pointing to a card propped up against the toaster. Hmmmmm. it says, "Scooter, I've gone out to lunch with my Uncle Henry, whom I haven't seen in many years. What a surprise! P.S. Randy's mother called about you boys going camping. I called your dad at work and he said it would be all right. There is a can of cookies on the cupboard for you."

"Yahoo! That's great!" I exclaimed. "By the way, who is Uncle Henry?"

"He's my mom's uncle. I saw him a few times when I was a little kid, but I don't remember him. He's the reason we're living here. He's owned this house for years, but didn't live here. He always rented it out and when my dad was laid off from his job in California, mom called Uncle Henry and he got a job for dad here in Ghost Lake and gave us this house to live in."

"Wow! That's what I call a good uncle!"

"Well, I guess he was more like a dad to my mom than an uncle. Her mom died when she was little and Uncle Henry and his wife took her in and raised her. His wife was my Grandma's sister."

"Why didn't your Grandpa raise her?" I asked.

"He was killed, back in World War I."

"Oh, I'm sorry." I said, not knowing what else to say. "It must have been rough for your mom, not having a mom or dad."

"Not really." Scooter said, "Uncle Henry and his wife raised her like a daughter. Mom has always said she had a happy childhood in California. She grew up there and we all lived out there until dad came back here to work."

"Do you miss California?" I asked.

"I thought I would, until I met you and now I'm having fun and I think I'm going to like it a lot. Which reminds me, it's not getting any earlier, we'd better get our stuff together and get going."

"Right! Let's get started."

A short time later we had Scooter's sleeping bag, tent, and can of cookies sitting on the back porch. Scooter made one last trip into the house and came out with a big grin on his face.

"What's so funny?" I asked.

"Nothing." Scooter declared, holding up two large firecrackers.

"Holy Cow! Where in the heck did you get those?"

"From my uncle." Scooter said. "The one that gave me the pup tent."

"What are you going to do with them?"

Scooter smiled a sinister smile. "They're what I call my aces in the hole, in case anyone or anything comes sneaking around the tent tonight."

"Ahaaa!" I said with realization of what he had in mind.

Scooter slipped the firecrackers into his pocket, picked up his tent and sleeping bag, and said. "Can you carry the cookies?"

Just as we were gathering up our gear, a car pulled into the driveway. Scooter's mom and a tall, white haired man stepped out.

"Hi mom!" Scooter called as he walked over and extended his hand. "You must be Uncle Henry.

I'm pleased to meet you."

Uncle Henry shook Scooter's hand and exclaimed. "By golly if you haven't grown up to be a big boy!"

I could tell Scooter's mom was proud of him as she said "Leonard is going into the sixth grade this year, Uncle Henry."

I looked at Scooter as he screwed up his face in disgust. "Mom." he whined, "Please don't call me that name, especially in front of my friends."

Scooter's mom laughed. "Oh all right dear, but it is your name and I'm sure Uncle Henry doesn't know you by Scooter."

Uncle Henry chuckled, "Well, Scooter is it? That's all right, I like nicknames. Mine was Boots, for the cowboy boots I used to wear."

Scooter turned to me. "And this is my friend, Randy, which is his nickname also."

Uncle Henry shook my hand. "How do you do Randy? I'm pleased to make your acquaintance. You can just call me Henry, I've haven't gone by Boots for many years."

I shook Henry's hand and smiled. "How do you do sir? Are you in town for a visit?"

"Yes," Henry said, "I came to visit my favorite niece and her family. I also came to bury a ghost."

It felt like my knees were going to turn to jelly! Did he say bury a ghost? I didn't think this day could get any stranger than it already had, but here was this old man talking about burying a ghost!

"What do you mean, Uncle Henry?" Scooter asked with a little tremor in his voice.

"Have you ever heard of the lost boy of Ghost Lake?" Uncle Henry asked.

"Yes." Scooter said. "In fact, we just heard about the story today. It sounds fascinating!"

"It is quite a story isn't it?" Uncle Henry said, "And it's all true, you see, Ghost Lake and I go back a long way. In fact, I lived in Ghost Lake before it was Ghost Lake."

"You did?" I asked. "Did you know the lost boy?"

"You might say I knew him quite well…The lost boy was my brother."

"What?" I exclaimed. "He was your brother?"

"Then you were the man in the library this morning!" Scooter exclaimed.

"You're the man offering the reward?" I asked.

It was Uncle Henry's turn to be surprised. "Why….how did you boys find out about that so soon? I've only talked to one person about it and that was just a couple of hours ago."

Scooter grinned in triumph. "We also know who the person was and where the conversation took place….It was Mrs. Randall at the public library."

Uncle Henry shook his head in amazement. "I'd sure like to hear how you boys came upon this information."

Scooter and I took turns relating the day's events and the story that Gramps had told us. We then told of how we went to the library to confirm the story and of how, when there, we were told of Uncle Henry and his reward offer.

"The thing I'm curious about, Uncle Henry," Scooter asked, "Is why you are willing to pay a hundred dollars reward for information?"

"Well now," Uncle Henry began, "Let me put it this way. I was only three years old when my brother disappeared. I can't remember anything about him and my parents never talked about him. In later years when I came back to Ghost Lake, I heard the story of how he disappeared and of how his ghost was supposedly roaming the woods. I tried to find his remains at that time, but was forced to give up after a short time, as I had a business back in California to attend to. I always meant to come back, but the years went by and this is the first chance I've had to pursue this seriously."

"I don't understand it, Uncle Henry," I said, "Why is it important to find his remains?"

"Well, after all, he was my brother. The least I could do for him is to give him a proper burial, and maybe that would put his poor ghost to rest."

"What do you think the ghost is looking for?" Scooter asked.

"Oh, I don't even know if there is a ghost and I would have no idea what it would be looking for if there was such a thing. I only know that my brother wandered into those woods over fifty years ago and never came back. If I could, I'd like to know why and what may have happened to him."

"Do you think we should still camp in those woods?" Scooter asked.

"I don't see why not." Uncle Henry said. "I've never heard of anyone having any harm come to them in that area. I sure wouldn't let a story stop me from having a good time."

"Thanks Uncle Henry." Scooter said with satisfaction. "That's exactly what we wanted to hear."

PACKING UP

❖ ❖ ❖

Scooter and I walked down the street to my house in a semi-state of shock. Not only was the legend apparently true, but we had actually met the brother of the ghost of Ghost Lake, or I should say the brother of the lost boy, as nobody had ever proved that there actually was a ghost. I shivered at the thought of Scooter and me in a tent in the middle of the night in the middle of the very woods the ghost was reported to be haunting.

I finally broke the silence that had fallen on both of us. "Scooter, I hate to admit it, but this idea of camping out doesn't seem to be as much fun as it did this morning."

"I know what you mean," Scooter admitted, "but I've been thinking. We've already told both our parents, Gramps, Uncle Henry, and last but not least, Arnold. Can you imagine what he'd tell the kids at school if we back out now? We'll be known as the Ghost Lake sissies for the rest of our life."

"I guess you're right." I had to agree, but deep in my heart I wished that Gramps had kept his mouth shut about the legend of Ghost Lake.

"Besides," Scooter said with a grin, "This makes me related to the lost boy through Uncle Henry, and I'm sure he'd never hurt us for that reason alone."

"I thought you said your mom was related through Henry's wife."

"She is, but that still makes me kind of a relative."

I wasn't about to argue with Scooter. I knew he was using this reasoning to convince himself that we would be safe. I too, had been thinking of reasons for not being scared.

"Maybe you're right, Scooter, and maybe there is no such thing, and maybe Arnold wouldn't make a big deal of it if we did back out."

"Well, here's your chance to find out." Scooter said, pointing up the street. Wouldn't you know it? Arnold was riding up the street on his bike, headed right toward us.

As he cruised to a stop, he looked over our tent, sleeping bag, and other gear. "Well, if it isn't the Girl Scouts of America!" He said with a laugh.

"Eat a rock, Arnold!" I said, surprising even myself.

"Oh wow!" Aren't we the tough guys!" Arnold said in mock fear. "Listen you guys, I'd like to ask you a favor."

Arnold almost sounded sincere in his request, so I curiously asked. "What kind of favor could we possibly do for you, Arnold?"

"I'd appreciate it if you wouldn't take any of the comics you're going to give me, with you in the woods tonight. I wouldn't want you crying all over the pages and staining them. Or maybe you'd tear the covers off when you're running out of the woods in the dark!"

Scooter and I did a slow burn as Arnold rode off on his bike, laughing wildly. I glanced at Scooter as he held on to Blanca's collar and snarled. "For two cents, I'd sic her on him!"

"That settles it!" I declared, "We stay all night! and I don't care if Frankenstein himself crawls into the tent!"

"For sure!" Scooter agreed, "Or Dracula, the Wolf man or the Creature from the Black Lagoon."

We were still laughing about that when we walked up the driveway to my house. I started carrying stuff out from my room, the garage and the basement. In a short time Scooter's tent and sleeping bag were buried under a pile of extra blankets, a box of food, four bottles of soda pop, comic books, a flashlight, and a small trench shovel. We were debating whether to take pillows or not when dad came home.

Stepping out of his car, he surveyed our pile of gear and said, "Are you boys running away from home or having a garage sale?"

"We're going camping." I said proudly, then added, "Oh dad, I'd like you to meet my new friend, Scooter Dobson. Scooter, this is my dad."

Scooter and dad shook hands while I turned my attention to the problem of how we were going to get this mountain of stuff to our camp site.

"Can you see anything we may have missed, dad?"

Dad walked over and began going through our pile. "What's in the food box?" he asked.

"Let's see," I said, trying to think of everything I had put in there. "There's hot dogs, ketchup, pork and beans, relish, and mustard."

"And," Scooter added, "Soda pop, potato chips, cookies, candy bars, and marshmallows."

"Hmmmmmm." Dad said thoughtfully, "How long are you staying?"

"Just overnight," I said, "Do you think we should bring bacon and eggs for breakfast?"

"No," Dad laughed, "I think you have enough junk food to last you for a while. You can come home in the morning and have breakfast."

"I guess we're all set then," I said.

"Just a minute. I think you need one more thing." Dad said as he went in the back door. He was back in a few minutes with a big forest green pack sack.

"Hey! That's just what we need!" Scooter exclaimed.

Dad smiled and began packing our pile into the pack sack. In Ten minutes he had transformed our jumbled pile into a neat package. He packed the small box of groceries on top, brought the flap over, and strapped it down. Picking up the pack sack, he handed it to me and said, "Do you think you can carry this?"

I struggled into the arm straps and lifted it up on my shoulders. It was heavy, but I felt I could handle it for the distance I had to travel. "Not too bad." I grunted.

"O.K.," Dad said, "How about some extra matches, another flashlight, and some mosquito repellent?"

"Good idea dad. We can just stick them in our pockets."

Mom came out on the back porch to say good-by. I could tell by the worried look on her face that she was trying to think of a reason for us not to go. "I still wish you boys would camp in the back yard. We could leave the back porch light on and you could come in during the night if you wished."

Half of me wanted to agree with her, but then I thought of Arnold and the consequences we would face if we chickened out. "No thanks, mom. We'll be all right. Don't worry; we'll be home right away in the morning."

"Now mother," Dad said, putting his arm around her shoulder, "There comes a time when all young boys have to go camping on there own and I think they're ready for it. They're getting to be big boys now and it's only for overnight."

"Well, I suppose." Mom said, "But you boys better be careful with the matches and campfire. Stay dry and warm and did you remember to bring pillows?"

"Yes mom, we'll be careful, and no, we don't need pillows. We'll roll up our jackets and sleep on them. Don't worry now. We'll be just fine."

"How about a good night kiss then?" Mom said, extending her arms.

I gave her a big kiss and a hug, shook dad's hand and waved as we started out the gate and down the street.

The sun had started to dip down toward the trees as we approached Ghost Lake Road. Our load of gear was beginning to take its toll, so we decided to stop and rest for a moment.

"Why don't you take a break and let me carry the pack sack for a while?" Scooter said.

"Why not?" I said, slipping out from the wide straps that had been cutting at my shoulders. "I'm sure glad we're not going on a five mile hike!"

Scooter slipped his arms through the straps and pulled the pack up on his back. "Hey! This is a load!" He exclaimed, "Remember, we have to pick up the rake and shovel we hid in the woods this morning."

"Oh yeah, I almost forgot. It was right down there under those evergreens." I said pointing to a grove of trees just up the road.

Ghost Lake Road seemed to be deserted at this time of the day. A faint light glowed from Gramp's kitchen window as we passed by his house. The only sound we heard was the distant hum of an outboard motor somewhere out on Ghost Lake. It was almost too quiet.

I told Scooter to wait on the road while I went to retrieve the hidden tools. I walked to the exact spot we had hidden them and circled the small clump of trees twice before the realization hit me. I ran back up to the road and waved Scooter over to the ditch.

"What's up?" he questioned.

"You're not going to believe this," I stated. "But the rake and shovel are gone."

"What do you mean, gone?" Scooter asked.

"I mean they are not here where we put them! Someone has stolen them!"

SETTING UP

❖ ❖ ❖

"It has to be Arnold!" Scooter exclaimed as we made our way up the path to our camp site. "Who else would pull a trick like that?"

I had to agree. Arnold was the only logical suspect. "He must have been spying on us when we hid the rake and shovel." I said.

"If he did," Scooter went on, "Then he may also have something up his sleeve for tonight, try to scare us or something."

"Yeah, you're right. I wouldn't put anything past him."

We entered our little clearing in the woods just as the sun was sinking below the trees. Looking around, I tried to determine if anything looked different from when we had left it. Arnold could have booby trapped the place or something. "We'd better hurry," I said, "We only have about an hour of daylight left, and we have a lot to do."

"Right!" said Scooter, "Why don't you start looking for some firewood and I'll set the tent up."

"O.K." I said, heading off into the surrounding woods in search of dead branches and old pine stumps. The woods were full of old blackened pine stumps, leftovers from the logging and forest fires of fifty years ago. These stumps were dry, full of pitch, and easy to pry out of the ground.

They also burned like a torch for a very long time. I was hoping I wouldn't have to go too far into the woods as I had an uncomfortable feeling about this place after all we had heard today. I shuddered to think that I had spent the last few days roaming around in these woods with no idea of the legend or the supposed ghost of the lost boy.

In a short time I returned to the camp site dragging several long dead limbs. Another trip into the woods produced some old pine stumps I had managed to uproot. A third trip finished off the necessary wood supply and all that was needed now was some birch bark and dry kindling.

"How's the tent coming, Scooter?" I called as I piled the firewood and kindling in the area of the fire pit.

"Not too bad," Scooter commented, "I tried to get all the sticks, stones and tree roots out from under the tent so it'll be more comfortable to sleep on."

"I'm glad you did that, Scooter. I wouldn't want to have to go to the doctor tomorrow and maybe spend the rest of the summer in the hospital."

Scooter looked at me with a frown and stopped pounding in the tent stakes. "What in tarnation are you talking about?" He asked.

"Why, haven't you heard?" I asked with a grin, "Sticks and stones may break your bones!"

"Ohhhhhhhh...sick!" Scooter groaned. "That has to be the corniest joke I've heard yet!"

"I thought it was pretty clever," I bragged. "By the way, do you need any help?"

"Yeah, stretch the tent tight while I pound the stakes in."

I grabbed the edge of the tent and began pulling. "It's not very big, is it?" I commented.

"It's big enough for us." Scooter said, pounding in the last of the stakes. Standing up he looked around the camp site and commented, "Boy, it sure looks different in the dark doesn't it?"

I could still see everything around us in the gathering twilight. "Heck! This isn't dark yet, another hour or so and then you'll see dark. Let's finish setting up camp before it really does get dark. We still have to dig a fire pit."

"O.K." said Scooter as he picked up two short poles, crawled into the flat tent, and proceeded to raise it up.

As Scooter crawled out of the tent, I questioned the sag in the middle. "It looks like it has a broken back," I laughed.

"Hold your horses!" Scooter exclaimed, "I'm not finished yet! I have to stake down the end ropes and that'll tighten up the sag in the middle."

He pounded in a short stake about six feet from either end and tied the end ropes to them. Just as Scooter had predicted, the sag almost disappeared and we were ready to move in. We dug our blankets out of the packsack, rolled out our sleeping bags, and crawled into the tent to arrange our beds.

Straightening out my bag, I laid back to try out the arrangement. With my head at the back of the little tent, I looked out toward the doorway and commented, "Are we going to have to sleep with these poles inside the tent?"

"Yes," Scooter said, "Unless you want to sit up all night and hold the tent up while I sleep. Just be careful you don't knock them over."

"O.K., but doesn't the door zip up?"

"Boy, you complain a lot!" Scooter teased. "No, it doesn't zip up. It has these little cloth ties that you tie to the front pole. You have to remember, this is an army surplus tent. It was made for tough soldiers, tenting out in the middle of some battle zone, not for some pansy tourists that can't handle a few mosquitoes."

"O.K...O.K., I'm not complaining, I was just wondering. Do you think this tent was really in a battle zone?"

"I don't know," Scooter said, thinking about that one, "But I'll bet if this tent could talk, it would tell us some pretty scary stories."

"Yeah, well, we wouldn't have time to listen right now anyway. We'd better get started on the fire pit."

"Why do we have to have a fire pit?" Scooter asked. "Can't we just build a fire on the ground?"

"I suppose we could," I answered, "But I think a fire pit would be a lot safer. I mean, it keeps the fire from spreading out and starting a forest fire. You always see fire pits in camp sites, and besides, it'll only take ten minutes or so."

"Well, let's get started then." Scooter said looking around at the deepening darkness. "It'll be dark soon and I don't want to be standing around here without a fire."

I picked up my little trench shovel and walked out in the center of our little clearing. "What do you think about this spot?" I said, pushing my shovel down into the dirt.

"It looks good to me." Scooter agreed.

We had been so busy setting up camp that neither of us had thought or mentioned the legend, or what we had learned. I was just about to dig the first shovel of dirt, when we were suddenly reminded of it all.

Blanca had remained in the background all this time, quietly watching us set up camp. We had almost forgotten about her, until now. With ears pricked forward, she uttered a low growl and slowly, step by slow step, cautiously made her way to the edge of the clearing. The hair on the back of her neck rose as she growled and peered into the darkened woods beyond.

Scooter nudged me and pointed at Blanca. He didn't have to explain to me what was happening. It was very clear that someone or something was out there, and Blanca didn't like it. I found myself holding my breath, waiting for I don't know what.

Scooter tip-toed over to where Blanca was standing. He kneeled down and put his arm over her, patting her side. "What is it girl? What's out there?"

Blanca turned to Scooter and whined low, then again turned to the woods and growled low, baring her teeth. I eased over by them and whispered, "What is it, Scooter?"

Scooter shrugged his shoulders, "I don't know, listen!"

From somewhere in the darkness beyond came the sound of a twig snapping and the faint rustle of leaves. I looked at Scooter. "Did you hear that?" he asked.

"I think so," I said, straining to hear and yet not really wanting to hear anything.

At that moment, Blanca decided to investigate further and took off, barking fiercely. "Blanca!" Scooter called, but too late, she had disappeared into the dark forest, leaving us all alone.

"Oh great!" I muttered. "It's almost dark. Our guard dog runs away, and we have no fire."

"C'mon!" Scooter said, "Forget the dumb dog! Let's get the fire going."

I returned to our selected place, grabbed the trench shovel, and began furiously digging a fire pit. I had only dug about eight inches deep when the shovel made a scraping, tinny noise.

"What was that?" Scooter asked.

"I don't know. I've hit something."

I scraped away some dirt from the object I had hit while Scooter ran back to the tent and returned with the flashlight.

"Shine it here, Scooter," I said pointing to the exact spot.

Scooter shined the light while I dropped the shovel and kneeling down, brushed the dirt away with my fingers.

"What the heck?" Scooter exclaimed as the light showed that we had struck something of metal or tin.

"What do you think?" I asked looking up at Scooter.

"I don't know, but it's getting dark and Blanca is still out there chasing who knows what. I think we should just build the fire on the ground and dig up the tin later."

"Good idea!" I said, as I hurried over to the firewood pile and gathered up some birch bark and small twigs for kindling. Placing the birch bark on the ground, I took a handful of small twigs and sticks and covered the bark. Scooter handed me a match and I struck it on a small stone and touched it to the birch bark.

A tiny flame licked at the edges of the bark, flared up, and caught on the tiny twigs. The tiny twigs burned up to ignite the larger sticks and in a few moments we had the beginning of a cozy campfire. As the flames grew higher, Scooter and I broke off larger pieces of the dead branches and added them to the fire.

Satisfied that it was going to burn, we stood up and admired our work. I was just about to comment on how cozy the fire was and what a difference it made in the atmosphere of our camp site, when Scooter broke my chain of thought.

Turning outward from the fire, he exclaimed, "Well, if it isn't the lost dog of Ghost Lake!"

We both laughed in relief as Blanca emerged from the darkness with her tongue hanging out. I know it sounds strange, but I swear she had a grin on her face.

"It doesn't look like she's scared or anything," I commented.

"Nahhhh! She was probably chasing a coon or a skunk or something," Scooter stated. "I told you she was a good guard dog, She ain't afraid of nothing!"

"Well, I'd prefer she stay here and guard, and forget about coons and skunks. I'm not worried about them."

"Yeah!" Scooter said holding Blanca's head in his hands and ruffling her ears. "Shame on you, girl, leaving us all alone in the dark!"

"Well, dogs will be dogs," I said. "Now, shall we cook supper first or dig up that tin thing I found?"

Scooter glanced at his watch. "I don't know. I'm kind of hungry, but not that much. It won't take that long to dig that thing up will it? Maybe it's a lost treasure or something."

"I was just thinking, "I said worriedly, "You don't suppose that tin thing is a berry pail, do you?"

Scooter's eyes grew wide as he realized the meaning of what I had just said. "You mean that maybe the lost boy's remains might be there too? I mean, like bones and stuff?"

SURPRISE!
❊ ❊ ❊

I hadn't thought about that. What if the lost boy's remains were here? But then, why would they be buried? Why wouldn't they be on top of the ground or at least just under the leaves? It didn't seem likely that we'd find any remains of anything, but then, you never know!

"I...I doubt it, Scooter. Remember what Gramps said about there being a lot of homesteaders around here, and loggers too? I'll bet it's an old can from someone's garbage or some kind of logging equipment dropped here many years ago."

"Well," Scooter said, "I guess we'll never know unless we dig it up. But if we hit some bones, I say we leave it, tell Uncle Henry about it and collect the hundred bucks."

"I don't know, Scooter. I wouldn't feel right collecting a hundred dollars from your great uncle for finding his dead brother's remains."

"Yeah, I guess you're right. It wouldn't feel right."

"We'll dig up the tin thing anyway and maybe that'll give us a clue of some kind."

As I walked over to the hole we had started, I glanced around the clearing and then up at the night sky. One or two stars twinkled in the last bit of lingering twilight. Night had officially fallen. This was it, I realized. We are finally alone and on our own. There's no light switch here to click on, no door to lock, and no mom or dad to call to.

Scooter shined the flashlight down into the hole as I fell to my knees and began scraping the dirt away from the tin. Brushing back the dirt, I uncovered what appeared to be a metal lid of some kind, about ten or twelve inches in diameter.

Scooter wrinkled his nose and shook his head, "I don't think it's a berry pail. Berry pails are a lot smaller than that."

"Yeah, but, maybe in those days they were a lot bigger."

"O.K., let's figure this out," Scooter stated. "The boy disappeared when, fifty or sixty years ago? Wouldn't you think a tin pail would have rusted away by now?"

"I don't know. I suppose it depends on how much moisture and stuff is in the ground."

"Well, I know one thing for sure," Scooter said. "We'll never know anything if we don't dig it up. Let's do it!"

"O.K." I said, picking up the trench shovel. "Let's dig around the edge and see if there's more under the cover."

I began digging around the edges of the lid and in a short time discovered that there was indeed, something under the cover. It appeared that it was either a metal pail or a large can of some kind.

Taking a breather, we sat by the edge of the hole and speculated as to what it might be, and how or why it came to be buried in this place.

"I don't think it belonged to the lost boy," Scooter stated. "Why would he want to bury a pail?"

"You're probably right," I agreed, then added, "Hey! You know what?"

"What?"

"Maybe there was a house or a homesteader's cabin around here in the old days. I've heard that lots of people in those days used to bury their money in their back yards because they didn't trust banks or were too far from any."

"Wow!" Scooter exclaimed. "Wouldn't that be something if that can is full of gold coins or even silver?"

We didn't have to be told to start digging! In another ten minutes we had dug all around the can, or pail, down to its bottom. The sides were brown with rust and worn through in several places. Scooter grasped the top with two hands and pushed it back and forth to loosen it from the soil.

"Hey, this thing is heavy!" he exclaimed. "Maybe it is full of gold!"

"Let me help you," I said, putting one leg down in the hole and grasping the pail around the bottom. With Scooter pulling and me lifting, we managed to get it up out of the hole and set it close to the fire.

We both sank to our knees and caught our breath, studying our anticipated treasure in the firelight. I added a few more sticks to the fire and the light revealed it was more like a can than a pail.

"Let's get the cover off!" Scooter said, rubbing his hands in anticipation.

"Right!" I said as I hooked my fingernails under the edge of the lid and tried to pull it off. "I think the lid is rusted on, it won't budge."

"Let me try," Scooter said, repeating the same procedure. "You're right," he said with a grunt, "It's rusted on tight."

"How about if I try to pry it off?" I said picking up the trench shovel.

"Give it a try," Scooter said. "What do we have to lose?"

I picked up the shovel and tapped the large can around the edges to loosen up the rust. I then punched a whole in the top of the lid with the tip of the shovel and pried back on the handle. It appeared to move a little.

"Wait!" Scooter exclaimed, picking up a stout stick. "I'll tap around the edges while you pry on it."

"O.K.," I said, pushing down on the shovel handle while Scooter tapped the edges with the big stick. He only gave it about ten taps when the rust gave way and the lid lifted a little on one side.

I dropped the shovel and said, "You lift from your side and I'll lift from mine." Hooking our fingers under the lid, we lifted and wiggled the lid up and down until it finally let loose with a sucking noise.

"Yeeeaak!" Exclaimed Scooter, as he stared at the contents of the can. "What in the heck is that?"

"I know one thing," I said with disgust. "It sure isn't gold!"

The can was filled to the brim with something that looked like thick brown syrup. Picking up a stick, I poked at the gooey material which seemed to have a crust covering it. I poked at the crust with some force and the stick broke through and sank into the taffy-like substance beneath.

"What is it?" Scooter questioned.

"I don't know," I said, pulling the stick out and holding it close to the firelight. "It looks like some sort of paste or something."

"Paste?" Scooter said, taking the stick. "Let me see." He pinched the material in his fingers and held it up to his nose. "It smells like grease or oil of some kind."

"Oil wouldn't be that thick," I said. "See if it burns."

Scooter thrust the end of the stick into the flames and within a second or two it began to burn rapidly. "It must be grease," Scooter stated.

"Who in the world would want to bury a can of grease?" I asked.

"Boy, you've got me," Scooter said in wonderment. "Maybe this was a logging camp and they used the grease for wagons and stuff."

"I don't know, and I really don't care," I said bitterly. "I thought for sure we had found a treasure of some kind."

"Yeah, what a bummer!" Scooter agreed. "But anyway, we can make some neat torches with this stuff."

He thrust the tip of the stick into the pail and twisting it, came up with a big blob of grease. Holding it to the flame, he produced a torch which lit up the entire clearing.

"Hey! That's cool!" I exclaimed, looking around for a stick of my own. I found a good one, about three feet long and two inches in diameter. "Perfect!" I said as I sunk the end of the stick into the grease can.

The stick sank down into the gooey grease about six inches and struck something solid. Not sure if I had felt it right, I pulled the stick back and poked it in again. Once more it bumped into something solid. Goosebumps prickled up on my arms.

"Scooter!" I exclaimed. "There's something hard down in that can!"

"What do you mean?" he asked.

Leaving my stick in the can, I said, "Feel it! Poke that stick up and down."

Scooter did as I said and exclaimed, "Hey! You're right! What the heck?"

At that moment Blanca once again began to growl and stare into the surrounding darkness. This time, instead of running off into the woods, she took two steps backward and stood between Scooter and me. It was different this time. I too could sense that something was out there watching us.

Scooter and I glanced at each other, not saying a word. I pulled my stick from the can and held it to the fire. As it caught, I raised it up high, trying to penetrate the darkness beyond. Scooter flicked on the flashlight, shining it along the edge of the clearing.

"I don't see anything, do you?" I asked.

"No, and I don't want to either," Scooter whispered back.

As suddenly as she had become alert, Blanca relaxed. She turned around twice, plopped down by the fire and laid her head between her paws.

"False alarm?" I questioned.

"I hope," Scooter added.

"C'mon, let's see what's in the can," I said, picking up the shovel and scooping out a large blob of grease. I scraped it off on one of the pine stumps and dug in for another scoop. About three scoops later I struck the object buried in the pail.

"What is it?" Scooter asked.

"I don't know," I said, poking at it with a stick. "It's all covered with grease."

"Grab it," Scooter said.

"You grab it!" I exclaimed. "Maybe it's some bones or something."

"Wait a minute," Scooter cried as he picked up the flashlight and ran over by the tent.

In a short time he returned holding something in his hand.

"What's that?" I asked pointing at the object.

"Rags," Scooter said. "The tent stakes were rolled up in these rags.

"What're you going to do with rags?" I asked.

"You don't think I'm going to stick my bare hand down in that gook, do you?"

"Ah hah!" I exclaimed, seeing what he was up to.

Scooter put his hand in the rag and then reached in the grease can and grasped the mysterious object. Grasping one end of it, he wiggled it back and forth, pulling upward at the same time. With a low, slurping, sigh, it came loose.

"What is it?" I asked anxiously as Scooter lifted the grease covered object from the can.

"I don't know, but it's kind of heavy," Scooter said holding it up in the firelight. "Hand me that other rag and we'll wipe off the grease."

I handed Scooter the rag and took a closer look at our find. It was covered with a thick coating of grease, making it impossible to identify. I was about to make a guess that it was some sort of cooking utensil, when Scooter realized what we had found.

"It's a gun!" he exclaimed.

"A gun? What?... What kind of gun?" I said in a hushed whisper.

Scooter wiped furiously with the rag. "Look, it's an old pistol! A revolver! An old six shooter!"

I held out my hand for the old revolver as Scooter wiped more grease off of it. "Let me hold it!"

"Be careful where you point it!" Scooter ordered. "It may be loaded."

"O.K., I'll check it out. I've seen in the movies where they open this little door on the back and turn the bullet holder to see if it's loaded." I then opened the little door and turned the bullet thing around. Looking in the door I could see that there were no bullets in it. "It's empty." I said, pointing it away from us. "Wow! Can you believe this?"

"Here," said Scooter handing me another rag. "Clean it up good."

With the clean rag, I managed to wipe most of the thick grease off. Only a slippery coating remained on the bluish-gray metal. Although the gun must have been buried here for many years, it apparently was none the worse for it. The can of grease had done its job well, protecting it from rain and snow for all these unknown years.

We sat by the fire and took turns rubbing it and cleaning the remainder of the grease off. After a while the excitement of our find cooled off and we began to reflect on how the gun could possibly have been buried here in the first place.

"I'll bet it's like you said before, Randy! There was probably an old house or cabin here and the owner buried the gun out in the back yard!"

"No...I don't think so Scooter," I argued. "Why would anyone bury a gun? Unless they robbed a bank with it or murdered someone."

I suddenly realized what I had said and the thought of it caused me to quickly hand the gun back to Scooter.

"Murdered?" Scooter said slowly, holding the gun in the flat of his hands. "Brrrrrr, I hope not!" He shivered as he laid the gun down on one of the clean rags.

I quickly sought to change the subject and the mood. "Oh well, we can figure it out later. I'm starved! Let's fix something to eat."

"Good idea!" Scooter said, just as anxious to change the subject as I was. "How would you like some hot dogs and beans?"

"Fantastic!" I said. "And some chips and pop."

Scooter opened the can of beans and set them close to the fire while I cut and sharpened a couple of hot dog sticks. It was not long before the beans were bubbling and hot dogs were turning on sticks held over the fire.

This was turning out to be the camping trip I had dreamed about. It was a beautiful night, sitting by the campfire cooking hot dogs, while reflecting on the day's events. Off in the distance, far out on Ghost Lake, a loon called its lonely wail.

Scooter too, had been reflecting on the day's events as he lay by the fire. "Say Randy?" He said as if the thought had just struck him. "Didn't that newspaper article at the library say that the lost boy was reported to have had a gun with him?"

I looked over at Scooter through the smoky campfire and my mouth dropped open!

COLT .44

❖ ❖ ❖

Scooter was right! In the excitement of finding the can and then the gun, I had forgotten all about the article or the lost boy! Now it all came back. I remembered that the article did say that the father believed that the boy had possibly taken a colt revolver with him. A chill ran over me as I realized that this was more than likely the gun that the lost boy had taken, and even worse, this was probably what the ghost of the lost boy was looking for!

I was almost positive, but I had to ask. "Scooter, Is that revolver a colt?"

"I don't know," Scooter answered. "Let's see if we can find some markings on it."

Scooter held the gun close to the fire and shined his flashlight on it. "Here, hold this, would you?" he asked, handing me the flashlight. "Shine it right here."

I held the flashlight on the gun as Scooter turned it over a few times and then began scratching on the barrel with his fingernail.

"Here it is!" He exclaimed. "It reads 44 cal. Colt!"

"Aaha!" I exclaimed. "So, it must be the lost boy's gun! I'll bet that's what the ghost has been looking for all these years!"

"Wait a minute," Scooter argued. "We don't know that for sure. There could be a lot of reasons for this gun being here."

"Like what for instance?"

"Well...like...ah...ah...dang it! I can't think of any right now, but I'm sure there must be some reason. Anyway, if it is the lost boy's, why is it buried and what happened to the lost boy?"

"Exactly Scooter, exactly," I said. "Why is it here and what happened to the lost boy? I don't think there's any question as to who brought that gun into these woods. It's why, how, and what that bothers me."

"I suppose you're right," Scooter admitted. "But, do you think that gun could have lain here all these years and not get rusty?"

"Sure!" I said with confidence. "Think about it. Does grease rot or rust or spoil? What better way to preserve something metal, than to bury it in grease?"

"But why did he want to bury it and preserve it?" Scooter questioned.

"There is the mystery!" I exclaimed. "Maybe after he had been lost for a while he knew he wasn't going to make it and buried the gun or maybe he figured his dad would really be mad if he was found with the gun."

Scooter walked over and put some more wood on the fire. Stirring up the coals with a long stick, he turned and said, "Do you really believe there's a ghost?"

I joined him by the fire, lying down, propped up on one elbow, I began breaking up a small twig and throwing it into the fire. "I guess I do," I finally said. "I mean if you look at what has been said by Gramps, Uncle Henry, the newspaper and the stories over the years, I mean, the fishermen who saw the boy described him correctly, and then there was the old lady who heard a kid crying in the woods. There's got to be something to it."

"Yeah, but that crying could have been anything," Scooter argued. "Coons, Skunks, owls, bears, who knows what."

I fell back on my back and let loose with a belly laugh. Scooter looked at me like I had just lost my marbles.

"What's so funny?" he asked.

I managed to stop laughing long enough to exclaim. "I was just picturing a skunk and a bear sitting in the woods crying."

Scooter smiled. "That would be funny," he admitted.

"But you're right," I assured him. "It could have been something else she heard, but what I can't figure out is, how come they never found his body?"

"Maybe a bear ate him, or ravens and crows or maybe somebody murdered him and buried him here close to the gun."

"That's it!" I exclaimed. "If someone murdered him, they'd bury the gun also to hide the evidence."

"But why in grease?" Scooter asked.

"Maybe the killer was going to come back later, when things cooled off and get the gun."

"Nah, that doesn't make any sense," Scooter declared.

"No, I guess not," I admitted. "Anyway, all this has been moving too fast. I'm totally confused and all this talk is giving me the creeps. Let's change the subject and enjoy the camping trip."

"Good idea," Scooter said lying back and staring up at the sky. Suddenly he sat upright. "Listen!" he exclaimed.

I listened, and over the low crackle of the fire came the far off distant rumble of thunder.

"Dang!" I said hitting the ground with my fist. "I'll bet we're going to get that rain my mom was talking about."

Scooter checked his watch. "It's almost nine o'clock. Maybe we should put the food box in the tent before it starts raining."

"Yeah, we can always lie in the tent and read comics by flashlight."

"And," Scooter said with a smirk, "after we meet Arnold in the morning, we'll have twice as many comics to read the next time."

"I can't wait to see his face when we come out of these woods in the morning," I said, laughing.

"What about the revolver?" Scooter asked. "Shall we bring it into the tent with us?"

"No way!" I exclaimed. "If there is a ghost and he comes looking for it, I don't want him in the tent with me!"

"Well, it's been out in the weather for fifty years or more," Scooter said. "I guess another night won't hurt it."

"Why don't we wrap it up in one of the grease rags and put it in the tent bag. That'll keep the rain off of it."

"O.K.," Scooter said, picking up the revolver. He hefted it in his hand and pointed it out toward the surrounding darkness. "Boy! If this old gun could talk, I'll bet it would tell some interesting stories!"

"That would be something, wouldn't it?" I agreed.

Scooter turned the gun over in his hands a couple of times, studying it in the firelight. "Hey!" he exclaimed.

"There's something carved on the handle! It looks like it may be someone's initials!"

"Let me see!" I said, hurrying over to where Scooter was standing.

"Get the flashlight," Scooter asked as he rubbed and scratched at the handle of the old revolver.

I shined the flashlight on the handle while Scooter rubbed and turned the gun toward the light.

"It looks like E.F., doesn't it?" Scooter said, holding the gun out toward me.

I studied the markings carefully. "It does, but it looks awfully worn. Who would E.F. be?"

"What was the lost boy's name again?" Scooter asked.

"I believe it was John Frankson, wasn't it?"

"Yeah, I think so. Well, the last initial matches anyway."

"It wouldn't be his initials anyway," I said. "Remember that the gun belonged to his father."

At that moment, a fat raindrop fell, striking me on the neck. Looking up at the sky, I held out my hand.

"Rain?" Scooter asked.

"Rain." I answered.

"C'mon," Scooter said, hurriedly wrapping the gun in the grease rag and placing it in the tent bag. "Grab the food box!"

I picked up the box of groceries and trotted over to the tent, pushed the box in, and crawled in behind it. Scooter was right behind me. Luckily there was a small space at the back of the tent where it came to a point. I shoved the box into the tiny space and set the flashlight on top of it.

"Not too bad," Scooter said as he turned and looked around our little shelter. "I'll just tie up the door flaps and we'll be as snug as two bugs in a rug."

I glanced up as I heard the first few drops tap on the canvas overhead. "Ah, Scooter," I asked. "Does this tent leak at all?"

Scooter's forehead wrinkled up as he searched for a way to tell me. "I don't think so, but I really don't know. I've never had it up before."

"What?" I exclaimed. "You've never had it up before?"

"No. I told you that my uncle gave me the tent just before we left. I never had a chance to try it out."

"Oh great!" I said, rolling my eyes. I could just see us sleeping in an inch of water.

A rapidly growing patter on the canvas announced the approaching rain. A bright flash overhead, accompanied by a tremendous thunder crash caused Scooter and me to jump six inches off the floor. We looked at each other in shocked terror as the sky opened up and a waterfall of rain poured down on our flimsy little tent. After a few minutes, we calmed down and Scooter shut the flashlight off to save the batteries. It was kind of cozy to lay back and watch the lightning flashes light up our dry little space.

It seemed that for once, Lady Luck had smiled on us. Only a few drops of water had made their way into the tent and already the rain had let up and settled into a steady patter.

Scooter snapped on the flashlight and shined it over the canvas overhead. "Pretty good tent, hey?" he bragged.

"Not bad Scooter, not bad," I admitted.

"So, what do you want to do?" Scooter asked. "Read some comics? Eat some cookies?"

"Both." I answered, reaching for the food box. "Shine the light over here."

"Just a minute. Let's peek out the door and see what it looks like." We crawled to the door and pulled back the flap. The rain had settled down and the thunder seemed to be retreating to the east. Only a few glowing embers remained of our fire and they were slowly losing out to the steady rain. We decided to remain in our snug tent and stay dry.

"This isn't as bad as I thought it would be," Scooter said, munching on a cookie.

"What do you mean?" I asked.

"Well, you know, I thought it would be a lot scarier than it is, with what we heard about the lost boy and the ghost and all that."

"Yeah, I know what you mean," I agreed. "I had imagined all kinds of things but even with the finding of the gun it doesn't feel scary."

Scooter laughed, "I'll bet Arnold is going to be mad in the morning when he has to cough up those comics!"

"It'll serve the jerk right!" I said, "But let's not count our chickens yet. The night is still young."

I lay on my back reading a superman comic while munching on a cookie. Listening to the patter of the rain, I smiled, thinking that this had to be the coziest feeling in the world.

Suddenly my heart jumped as something touched my leg! I thought for sure it was the ghost of the lost boy until Scooter sat up with a cookie and reached toward the door.

"Here girl," he said, handing a cookie to Blanca, who lay with her head and front shoulders under the tent flap, one paw resting on my leg.

"What is this?" I said. Acting insulted. "You never said anything about sharing the tent with a dog."

"Ahh, c'mon, Randy," Scooter pleaded. "It's wet and cold out there, and Blanca's afraid of the thunder. I'll keep her down by my feet."

"O.K., O.K.," I said giving in. Actually, I was secretly happy that she would be in tent with us. I felt a little safer with her so near. "Here girl," I said, giving her half a cookie.

That was a mistake. I should have known that she wouldn't be satisfied with only half a cookie. No sooner had I settled back down with my cookie and my comic, when I felt her slowly inching her way up between Scooter and me. I tried to ignore her, but she looked at me with her big, sad, brown eyes and placed her paw on my shoulder.

I lowered my comic book and looked at her with disgust. She tipped her head to one side and pricked her ears up. Her unspoken expression asked, "Could I have one more cookie, please?"

I pretended not to pay any attention to her. I kept on munching my cookie and turning the page on the comic. Blanca did not give up easily. I saw her out of the corner of my eye as she inched up once more. I was about to scold her as I lowered my comic, but she beat me to the punch. She reached over and licked my neck. This was the last straw!

"You know, Scooter," I commented. "It's not too bad braving the hardships of sleeping on the ground, putting up with a few mosquitoes, or even the rain storm. But, I draw the line when a wet, smelly dog lies down by my side, breathes her bad breath in my face, licks my neck, and eats my cookie."

Scooter grinned, knowing I was kidding. He reached over and put his arm around Blanca, pulling her to him. "C'mon girl, I'll give you a cookie."

In a few moments Blanca was fast asleep and our eyelids were beginning to droop also. I had planned on staying up late; enjoying every minute of the camping trip, but the fresh air and the long day took their toll.

"I can't stay awake anymore," I admitted. "I'm going to turn in."

"Me too," Scooter said, shutting off the flashlight. "Good night."

"Good night," I mumbled, wiggling down into my sleeping bag.

Night sounds drifted over our little camp site like the ghost of the lost boy. From far out in the distance, somewhere on Ghost Lake, a loon called its lonely wail. I tried to picture what Ghost Lake must look like at night. I visualized a smoky mist rising from the dark water and drifting toward a rocky shore. Slowly, out of the mist came a shadowy figure of a young boy, carrying a berry pail and an old revolver.

I shuddered and shook my head to try to clear the image. In the dark, Blanca moaned low, sighed and squirmed closer to the warmth of our bodies.

GHOST ATTACK

❧ ❧ ❧

I felt it before I heard it, a low, deep, rumble of a growl. My ribs tingled with the sensation of vibration. I had been sleeping so soundly that upon wakening, I was unaware as to where I was. In a few seconds my head cleared and I realized with a start that the deep growl I was hearing came from Blanca, lying beside me. For a moment I was paralyzed by fear, feeling for sure that the ghost of the lost boy was standing right outside our tent. Reaching over Blanca, I frantically shook Scooter.

"Scooter! Scooter! Wake up!" I whispered hoarsely, "He's here, Scooter! He's here!"

Scooter pushed up on one elbow and rubbed his head. "Huh? What? What?" he mumbled. "What the heck are you talking about?"

"The ghost!" I said with a shiver. "Listen to Blanca!"

At that moment Blanca confirmed what I had said by baring her fangs and changing her growl to a full fledged snarl. Scooter flicked on the flashlight, shining it on Blanca, but she never changed her tone or took her eyes from the tent flap.

"You see what I mean?" I said with wide eyes. "She senses that he's out there!"

"Did you see him?" Scooter whispered.

"No, but I'm sure it's him. Remember what Gramps said about animals having a sixth sense?"

"Well yeah, but if you didn't see anything, maybe it's just some small animal, like a coon or rabbit."

"I doubt it," I argued. "She wouldn't growl like that at a small animal. Why don't you take the flashlight and check it out?"

"Forget it!" Scooter exclaimed. "I'm not going out there!"

"Then send Blanca out there! We can't just sit here and wait for it to attack us!"

"Good idea!" Scooter exclaimed as he turned the light toward the flap and placed his hand on Blanca's shoulder. He gently pushed her toward the door. "Go get'em girl! Sic em!" Blanca didn't move. "C'mon girl, go! Get em"

Blanca wouldn't budge. Scooter went through his vocabulary, looking for the magic words. "Attack!... Kill!... Charge!... Bite!"

It was no use. Whatever was out there lurking in the dark, Blanca wanted no part of it. Dropping to her belly, she looked back at us and whined. Scooter looked at me with futility, not knowing what to say or do.

"Now what do we do?" I whispered with a little fear in my voice.

"I don't know," Scooter said with a frown. "She sure doesn't want to go out there."

"I thought you said she wasn't afraid of anything." I asked.

"I didn't think she was," Scooter said in Blanca's defense, "But then, she probably has never run up against a ghost before either."

I was tempted to holler for help or scream, but I managed to control myself and ask. "Now what do we do? We're trapped in here!"

"I've got it!" Scooter exclaimed, snapping his fingers. "I'll throw the firecrackers!"

"You think a ghost is afraid of firecrackers?"

"What have we got to lose?" Scooter said, digging in his pants pocket.

I dug in my pocket and came up with two stick matches and handed them to Scooter. "Here, one for each."

"How should we do this?" Scooter asked.

"Hmmmmm," I said, thinking. "How about if we twist the two fuses together for a double bang?"

"Good idea!" said Scooter, "And I'll hold the tent flap open with one hand and throw with the other. You light the fuses!"

"O.K.," I said, "But I was just thinking. What if it doesn't work? What then?"

"We'll worry about that later," Scooter said, twisting the two fuses together. He then grabbed the tent flap. "Ready...fire one!"

I scratched a stick match along the zipper of my pants and it flared into a flame. Slowly I brought the match to the entwined fuses Scooter held out to me. For an instant nothing happened, and then the fuses sputtered, smoked, and began burning rapidly.

Scooter quickly thrust his hand through the tent flap and gave our ghost grenade a fling into the darkness. For a brief moment there was complete silence. Suddenly from out of the dark mist came a crashing Barooom!...Barooom!

I can't recall exactly what happened in the next few moments, but I do remember it was sheer terror and total confusion on my part, as I was sure we were under attack by some monster of one sort or another.

Looking back in a cooler frame of mind, I seem to remember Blanca leaping back at the sound of the blast. In her desperate attempt to escape, she charged to the back of the tent, knocking down the rear support pole that Scooter had warned me about. Apparently he forgot to mention it to Blanca, as she broke it completely in half in her lunge for safety.

Everything happened so fast that we didn't have a chance to react. Blanca reversed herself when the rear of the tent collapsed and charged backward into me and Scooter, knocking us down and the front support pole with us. Now we were in trouble!

In a desperate attempt to save the tent from falling in, Scooter and I pushed upward on the canvas. Not realizing our strength or taking into account the rain soaked ground, we pushed too hard and uprooted the tent stakes, our last hope of support.

Blanca at this time, chose to make a rapid exit and in doing so, knocked Scooter and me over, collapsing the tent around us like a huge, wet sack.

Scooter and I fell in a crumpled heap among the overturned grocery box, broken tent poles, sleeping bags, and comic books. With sheer terror in our hearts we lay there not moving, feeling for sure that at any moment we would feel the sharp claws and bulky weight of the huge creature that must be lurking over us at this very instant. With the return of our breath came the realization that we were still alive and as of yet, nothing had pounced on us.

"Scooter," I whispered. "Are you O.K.?"

"Yeah, I'm fine...How about you?"

"O.K., I guess...What the heck happened?"

Scooter raised the fallen canvas with one hand and retrieved the fallen flashlight. He turned to me with a grin and said, "There's one thing Blanca is more afraid of than thunder."

"Wait a minute!" I interrupted. "Let me guess...firecrackers?"

We both fell back laughing, not only at Blanca and our predicament, but for the sheer joy of still being alive.

In a short time we came to the conclusion that we couldn't spend the rest of the night like this. Neither of us wanted to suggest going outside to set the tent back up, but we had to do something.

"Now what do we do?" I questioned.

"I suppose we'll have to cut some new tent poles. Shall we take a look outside?"

"I guess so," I said, digging my flashlight out from the mess at the back of the tent.

With the tent draped over our backs, we crawled to the front and untied the tent flaps. Peering out, we shined our flashlights around the tiny clearing. The rain had stopped and a misty fog had settled in, creating smoky tunnels of light for our flashlights. The campfire was completely out and the only sound was the faint dripping of water from the rain soaked leaves.

"I wonder where Blanca is," I whispered.

"I don't know," Scooter answered.

"Try calling her."

"Blanca. Here girl," Scooter called in a low voice.

"C'mon Scooter, you can call louder than that."

"Blanca! Here girl!" Scooter half-shouted.

"There she is!" I said as my flashlight picked up the glow of her eyes as she entered the clearing. "C'mon girl!"

"Good girl! Good girl!" Scooter exclaimed as he ruffled her neck and ears. "You didn't leave us, did you?"

"Well," I stated. "If she came back, it must be safe to get out of the tent. Let's go cut some new tent poles and get set up again."

"Right," said Scooter. "We can cut two poles from that brush pile we made."

"Let's go!" I said, crawling out onto the damp, soft, ground.

Standing up, we shined our flashlights around the clearing again to make sure it was safe. We then made our way over to the brush pile and selected two poles much like the ones we had broken. We then pounded in the tent stakes again and Scooter crawled in and raised the tent with the new poles.

"Hey! Hey! We're back in business!" Scooter called from inside the tent as the second pole was raised. "Shine your light in here and I'll tidy up a bit."

I held back the tent flap and shined the light in while Scooter picked up the scattered comics and groceries and straightened out the sleeping bags.

"Looks good, Scoot," I commented as he backed out of the tent.

"Good enough," Scooter said as he rubbed his hands and looked around the clearing. "What do you think, Randy? Should we start up the fire again?"

The thought of a warm crackling fire sounded great. I had gotten a chill standing out in the damp night. "Good idea! Let's see if there's any dry wood."

We gathered up some bark, twigs and sticks as we had before and struck a match to it. The bark sputtered and began to burn feebly, but the wood was damp and would not catch at all. Scooter knelt down and began blowing on the burning bark, trying to create a draft, but it was no use. It was simply too wet.

"No such luck," I said. "It's not going to burn. We might as well get back in the tent and warm up in our sleeping bags."

"Yeah," Scooter agreed. "These mosquitoes are getting bad. Do we have any more of that repellent?"

"I think we put it in the tent bag with the revolver when we went to bed," I said.

"I almost forgot about the revolver with all the excitement we had," Scooter said as he walked over to the tent bag.

Kneeling down, Scooter groped in the tent bag. Suddenly he began to rapidly move his hand around in the bag.

"What're you doing, Scoot?" I asked.

Scooter sat back and held open the tent bag. "Randy!" he croaked with a little tremor in his voice. "The gun is gone!"

STAY OR GO
❖ ❖ ❖

"C'mon Scooter," I complained. "Quit fooling around! Let's get back in the tent. It'll be daylight in a few hours."

Scooter, looking like he had seen a ghost, walked quickly up to me, grasped my upper arm and whispered, "I wish I was kidding, but I'm not! The gun is not in the bag!"

Scooter had to be teasing! I ran over to the bag, picked it up and shook it upside down. Out tumbled one small bottle of insect repellent. My mind raced as I tried to figure out what this meant. There was only one conclusion. Someone or something had taken the gun!

This also meant that someone or something must be at this very moment, lurking in the dark woods nearby.

I tried to think quickly of what we could do or where we could go. I just knew I didn't want to be in this place at this time. What I wouldn't have given for the sun to suddenly pop over the trees and light up this dark, damp night.

Confusion and fear ran through my mind as Scooter broke into my thoughts.

"Now what do we do?"

"I don't know, Scooter. I don't know. What do you think?"

Scooter shook his head. "I don't know either, but I'll tell you one thing. I'm freezing out here.

Let's go back in the tent and figure out what to do."

"O.K." I said as I shined my flashlight around the clearing one more time.

We crawled into the tent and called Blanca in with us. I don't know why, but for some reason I felt more comfortable in the tent. We crawled into our sleeping bags to warm up and discuss this latest development. The warmth of the sleeping bag and Blanca snuggled up against us made me feel much better. I wasn't nearly as shaky as a few minutes ago.

Scooter, the master planner, broke the silence by suggesting that we only had two options. "As I see it, we can do one of two things. One, we can stay here and tough it out. There are only a couple of hours until daylight. Two, we can take our flashlights and try to follow the path back out to the road."

Neither choice thrilled me, but I had to admit it, Scooter was probably right. I tried to think of some other options, but came up with a blank.

"I guess if I have to vote," I began, "I'll vote for staying here and I'll tell you why. I feel safer in the tent. It's warm and dry. We still have Blanca for a guard dog, and last but not least I'm not crazy about going out into the cold, damp night and trying to find the path while not knowing what is lurking in the dark woods."

"Yeah." said Scooter, "And don't forget our bet with Arnold! Also, I don't think that whoever or whatever took the gun is interested in us or it would have done something when it had the chance. Now that it has what it came for, I think it'll leave us alone."

"Will you stop calling it 'it'!" I said with a shudder. "You make it sound like a creature from a science fiction movie!"

Scooter grinned. "I'm sorry, but if whatever is still out there, I don't want to be stumbling around out there in the dark with only a little flashlight."

"Which reminds me," I added, "Why don't we go out and get the hatchet and machete and bring them in here with us."

"Good idea," Scooter said, crawling out of his sleeping bag. "Let's go get them."

"Well, we don't need two people to carry a hatchet and machete. I'll stay here and shine the flashlight out for you. Blanca might run away again if we both go."

Scooter exclaimed. "I'm not that dumb! If I go out there, you're going with me!"

At the risk of being called a chicken, I had to agree. "O.K. O.K., I'll go with you, but I get to hold the light."

We poked our heads out the flap of the tent and I shined the flashlight around the clearing. Wisps of fog rose from the wet ground as rain drops still dripped from the bushes and trees. All that was left of our once roaring campfire was a small mound of wet, grayish black ashes. Leaning against a small stump on the other side of the fire pit were the hatchet and machete.

"There they are!" I whispered, shining the foggy beam at the wanted items.

"Ready?" Scooter asked.

"Ready."

We crawled out quickly, jumped up and made a mad dash across our little clearing. Scooter grabbed the hatchet and I grabbed the machete. Sliding through the mud and wet grass, we made it back to the tent in less than twenty seconds and dove in through the door flap.

Once our heartbeats and breath had returned to normal, I turned to Scooter and said, "Maybe we should just stay up for the rest of the night. It would only be for a couple of hours."

"I thought of that." Scooter said, "But I don't know if I want to stay up and worry about all that's happened, and besides, I'm beat. Blanca will wake us up soon enough to grab the hatchet and machete."

Once again I had to admit that Scooter was probably right, but I wasn't too sure I'd be able to sleep with the thought of the lost boy's ghost drifting around our campsite.

"Let's shut the lights off and save the batteries," Scooter suggested. "We may need them again before the nights over."

"Right." I said, shutting off my flashlight. I lay back down and silently hoped that we wouldn't have to use them again. I wished that I could just close my eyes and open them to a bright sun and chirping birds.

Blanca moaned in her sleep and twitched her leg. Overhead, the tree tops whispered in the breeze and in the tent a lone mosquito hummed his warning song. All was quiet. In spite of my wanting to stay awake, my eyelids began to droop as drowsiness overcame me.

Scooter broke the silence. "Randy? You awake?"

"Mmmmmmm, Yeah Scooter. What is it?"

"I was just thinking. How did whoever or whatever know that the gun was in the tent bag?"

That was a good question! I suddenly sat up, fully awake! "That's right Scooter! Whoever it was must have been watching us when we dug up the gun and hid it in the bag."

"Exactly!" Scooter exclaimed.

"Remember when Blanca took off into the woods the first time? I'll bet there was someone out there watching us!"

"Or some...thing." I added soberly.

"What do you mean by that?" Scooter asked, flicking on his flashlight.

"I mean, with the stories about the ghost of the lost boy and all that, I was just wondering..."

"No," Scooter said seriously. "There's got to be a better explanation than that."

"How about Arnold?" I asked. "Maybe he sneaked up on us and stole the gun to scare us or just to be mean. He'd do anything to win the bet!"

Scooter giggled. "Yeah, and I'll bet that's who Blanca was chasing through the woods that last time! He's probably in the next county by now."

We both had a good laugh at the thought of Arnold running through the dark woods with Blanca in hot pursuit. We felt a little better now, thinking that we knew what had happened. With our minds more at ease, we snuggled back down and relaxed.

As much as we would have liked to forget it, the ghost question was still unanswered. I don't know why, but Scooter looked upon me as some kind of an authority on ghosts.

"Randy, what do you think? Do you really think there could be such a thing as a ghost of the lost boy?"

"Well," I began. "Let's look at the facts.

We know there was a lost boy and it's most likely that the old gun we found belonged to him or his dad. So I guess that it's possible that his ghost could be wandering around.

Scooter slowly shook his head. "I don't know. We've been over this before and it still doesn't make sense to me. Someone made a special effort to preserve that gun in grease, so they must have been planning to come back for it, but didn't. Why I don't know, and I doubt if we'll ever find out the reason behind it."

"I guess that's why I believe in the ghost," I said. "They say that people become ghosts when their spirit can't rest. If the lost boy died and his spirit couldn't rest because of the gun or some other reason, then he probably became a ghost and couldn't rest until his problem was solved."

"I don't know if that makes any sense either." Scooter argued.

"Well, I can't explain it. You asked me if I believed in the ghost. You didn't ask me to prove it."

Scooter yawned a huge yawn. "Well, ghost or no ghost. I'm going back to sleep."

"Good idea," I commented as I turned over and snuggled against Blanca. Somewhere in the night beyond, a chorus of bullfrogs started croaking and singing. I felt cozy and tired and not scared anymore.

FOREST FIRE?

❖ ❖ ❖

True to Scooter's word, Blanca, the ever watchful guard dog woke us up once again. This time though, it was not with a growling snarl, but a soft, pleading whine.

Scooter woke up first and gave me a poke. "Randy, wake up! Blanca's whining."

It seemed as I had just fallen asleep. I was warm and snug in my sleeping bag and sleeping soundly. I did not want to wake up, least of all for a whining dog. "Mmmmmm-mm..." I mumbled, "Maybe she has to go to the bathroom. Let her out."

"I don't think so," Scooter whispered. "I think it's getting daylight. There's a glow outside."

"What time is it?" I asked.

Scooter looked at his watch. "It's almost three thirty."

"It's too early for daylight," I said, opening my eyes. "Besides, I don't see any glow."

"Yes there is!" Scooter insisted. "Look out by the tent door."

I leaned up on one elbow and looked toward the doorway. Scooter was right! There was a glow outside, but it flickered dim and then bright. "Hey!" I whispered. "That's not daylight! It looks like the glow of fire."

"Forest fire?" Scooter asked.

"Nah," I said, sitting up. "No forest fire would burn after the rain we had tonight. We couldn't even get our campfire to burn after the rain."

"Yeah, that's right." Scooter agreed, turning his head, "Shhh...Listen!"

I strained my ears to listen. I could barely hear it, but it was definitely the faint snapping and crackling of fire. Scooter looked at me with a questioning look. I shrugged my shoulders in answer as the glow grew brighter. Blanca chose this moment to get up and slowly slide under the tent flap in silence.

"Oh great!" I muttered. "There goes our guard dog again."

Scooter reached over and picked up his machete. "Get ready!" he ordered.

I picked up the hatchet and held it by my side, not sure of what I would do if I had to use it. Scooter must have been more scared than I was as he held the machete poised to swing at the first thing that moved.

"Put that down Scooter!" I cautioned. If you swing that thing in here you'll take my head off, or at least an arm or a leg."

Scooter lowered the machete, but continued to watch the tent flap, ready to spring in an instant. "O.K., but if something comes through that door...you'd better be ducking!"

The reddish glow continued to grow brighter and now we could hear the definite snaps and pops of a real fire.

Blanca had not returned and we hadn't heard a sound from her. I knew we couldn't wait another hour or so for daylight, but I also felt we had to do something.

Finally Scooter broke the silence. "Let's take a peek out there and see what's going on."

"I don't know Scooter," I said reluctantly. I wasn't sure if I wanted to see what was out there.

"Well, I don't think ghosts build fires, and besides, we can't just sit here for the rest of the night. If it is a forest fire we're going to have to run for it."

"I guess so," I agreed. "Let's take a peek."

Scooter leaned forward and untied one side of the tent flaps. Turning to me, he motioned with his hand for me to look with him.

I crawled up to the front of the tent and waited. Scooter looked at me. "Ready?" he whispered.

"Ready."

Scooter slowly pushed back the tent flap and folded it back over the tent. Together we leaned forward and slowly poked our noses out the doorway.

What we saw was not frightening...but, it sure added to the mystery. Scooter and I looked at each other with wrinkled foreheads and open mouths.

Our campfire was burning brightly! Not only that, but there curled up by the fire, the picture of comfort, was Blanca!

"What the heck?" Scooter asked, looking at me.

"Don't ask me." I countered.

Scooter nudged me with his arm and nodded toward the far side of the clearing. A figure stepped out from the shadows and walked toward the fire with an armload of sticks. Blanca didn't move, bark, growl, or snarl. The figure dropped the sticks and then squatted down and added one or two to the fire.

"Who's that?" Scooter whispered.

"I can't tell," I whispered back. "I think it's a man and he's definitely alive, not a ghost."

The man warmed his hands by the fire and then turned and began petting Blanca and scratching her ears. She in turn, looked up and him and licked his hand.

"Good guard dog!" I whispered sarcastically.

"She must know him," Scooter argued, studying the man.

"I wish he'd turn this way so we could see who he is," I added.

"Hey!" Scooter said, sticking more of his head out the doorway." Isn't that the old man we talked to this morning?"

"Gramps?" I asked, sticking my head out.

"Yeah, Gramps," Scooter said.

I studied the figure intently. It did look like Gramps in the dim light, but what in the world would he be doing here at this time of the night?

"Is it him?" Scooter asked.

I...think so," I answered, "But, I'm not positive."

"Say hello or something," Scooter whispered. "He knows you."

Here goes nothing, I thought to myself. "Gramps?" I called out. "Is that you?"

The man turned in the firelight and I could see that it indeed was Gramps.

"Hello boys!" he called back. "You going to stay in that damp tent all night or come warm up by the fire?"

Scooter looked at me questioningly.

"Let's go." I whispered. "And leave the machete here."

We crawled out of the tent, stood up, and walked over to the fire, still wondering what was going on. Gramps continued scratching Blanca's ears like it was the most natural thing to do and Blanca just sat there, enjoying every minute of it.

This was really getting strange. What do you say to someone who walks into your camp at three in the morning?

"Uhh...how did you get the fire started Gramps?" I said for lack of anything else to say.

"Easy," Gramps said. "I took some of that grease you boys have in that can, smeared it on some birch bark and it took right off."

Swell, I thought to myself. He had to find the can of grease. Now how were we going to explain that? It isn't every day that you see two twelve year old boys lugging around a huge can of grease.

Scooter must have been thinking along the same lines as he dreamed up a good whopper. "Oh yeah," he began. "We figured that grease would come in handy for fire starting, so we hauled it up here in the woods."

Gramps looked at us with a hint of a smile. "Good idea," he said. "But, I haven't seen grease come in a can like that for fifty years or so. Where'd you ever find it?"

"Oh my dad had it in his garage for years and years," Scooter said with confidence. "I think he inherited it from some old relative or something."

Boy, this kid could really lay it on thick! I could tell he wasn't fooling Gramps, so I tried to change the subject.

"By the way Gramps, what are you doing up in these woods at this time of the night?"

"Well, I knew you boys were going to be camping out tonight, so I thought I'd drop by and see how you're doing. Have you had any problems or anything strange happen?"

I glanced at Scooter. How much should we tell? "Oh, nothing that we couldn't handle." I didn't think that was a lie. After all, we were still alive and kicking.

"Well, I heard your dog barking a while back and then what sounded like two gunshots. So, I figured I'd come and take a look. I had just gotten my pants on and stepped out the door when I saw that Barnswell kid tearing down Ghost Lake Road with your white dog right on his tail."

"Arnold?" I asked.

"I guess that's his name. Anyway, I whistled to your dog and she came over to me, but that Barnswell kid was setting a new world record for the two mile run."

"Is that when you came up here then?" Scooter asked.

"No, that was a couple of hours ago. I figured that he must have been up to no good and you had probably set the dog after him, so I thought you were safe, and I went back to bed. I tossed and turned for a long time, but couldn't go back to sleep, so I got up, made some coffee, and then decided to come and check on you boys."

"So!" I said laughing with Scooter. "It was Arnold that Blanca was chasing! Man, what I wouldn't have given to have seen that!"

"What about the gunshots I heard?" Gramps asked.

Scooter and I laughed again. "Those weren't gunshots, Gramps," I explained. "Those were two big firecrackers that we lit off."

"I see." Gramps said. "So, nothing happened then?"

"Not really," I lied. I could tell Gramps knew more than he let on and I could also tell that he knew that we knew more than we were letting on. He was definitely fishing for more information.

Scooter sensed it also and began a little fishing expedition of his own. "Say Gramps, could you tell us a little more about the story of the lost boy?"

I don't know why, but Gramps sort of evaded the question.

I could tell he was in a different mood than he was in when he told us the story the first time. "Hmmff," he said. "Not much to tell. The boy got lost and nobody ever found him. He never showed up again."

I shot Scooter a questioning glance as Gramps got up and rolled a log over by the fire. He sat down and began filling his pipe. Reaching over, he pulled a stick from the edge of the fire and held the glowing tip to his pipe. He seemed in another world as he stared at the fire with a blue haze of pipe smoke floating over him.

I shivered as I looked at him by the fire. He had almost a ghost-like appearance with his white hair and gnarled old hands. I wondered if he was telling us all he knew or if he had made some of it up.

Scooter had one thing on his mind, the hundred dollar reward that Uncle Henry was offering. He persisted in his questioning. "Gramps, how could anyone convince someone else that the lost boy existed? I mean, other than what was in the newspaper."

Gramps continued staring at the fire. "You couldn't convince anyone," he finally said. "Besides, it was so long ago that hardly anyone knows about it or cares, and there isn't a lick of proof of anything."

We had the proof in the revolver, I thought to myself, or at least an important clue. Now that was gone and we'd probably never find out what happened.

I sat down by the fire, only to discover that the ground was still damp. "Yuk!" I said jumping up again.

"What's the matter, Randy?" Scooter asked.

"The dang ground is still wet!" I answered, rubbing the seat of my pants.

"Wait," Scooter said, walking around the fire. "I'll get the tent bag and we can both sit on it."

Scooter picked up the tent bag, hefted it a couple of times, then looked at me with wonder. Holding the bag with his left hand, he reached into it with his right and slowly pulled out the once lost revolver.

Gramps' white eyebrows rose. "What in tarnation have you got there?"

I grinned from ear to ear. "That is our proof of the lost boy's existence!" I said, not having the slightest idea of how it got back in the tent bag.

Scooter turned the gun over a couple of times and smiled. "Somehow this feels more like a crisp one hundred dollar bill to me," he laughed.

LOST BOY FOUND

❖ ❖ ❖

I looked at Scooter standing there, holding the old Colt revolver. The cat was out of the bag.

Our secret find was in the open. It had to happen sooner or later and I guess Gramps was as good a person to share our secret with as any. After all, he was the one who let us in on the story of the lost boy in the first place.

Scooter walked over with the old Colt and the tent bag. I took the tent bag and spread it out, making room for both of us to sit. I held out my hand and Scooter placed the revolver in it. I still couldn't believe that we had gotten it back!

I looked over at Gramps and he still had that faraway look in his eyes. "I guess we have some explaining to do Gramps. I imagine you're wondering what's going on."

"Yes, I'd like to hear your story from the beginning," he said.

I began with how I had been playing in the woods and had met Scooter. I told of how we had begun to clear around the tree fort and had gotten the idea for a camp-site.

"And you had never heard of the legend of the lost boy until this morning?" Gramps asked.

"That's right," I said. "Neither of us had ever heard any-thing about it until we talked to you this morning."

Scooter put in his two cents worth. "Yeah, you're story really freaked us out. We would have probably chickened out on the camping trip, but we had already bet Arnold fifty comic books that we'd spend the night. So, we didn't have any choice but to go through with it."

"I see...," Gramps said.

I jumped back in and told Gramps of how when we had dug the fire pit, we accidentally discovered the can of grease and the revolver in it. I explained about the news-paper article mentioning that the lost boy had taken a re-volver with him and that it was our idea that this was the very revolver.

"It has to be his!" Scooter exclaimed. "Who else would it belong to?"

"We think Gramps..." I said, pausing for a dramatic ef-fect, "That the lost boy was most likely murdered with this revolver and then the killer buried the gun to hide the evi-dence. The only thing we can't figure out is why he would bother to preserve it in grease."

"Go on," Gramps said. "What happened after you found the old gun?"

Scooter went on to tell of the thunderstorm and Blanca disappearing into the night. "And when we came out of the tent the next time...the gun was gone!"

I then told of how we had been awakened by Blanca's whining and the glow of the fire. "You know the rest Gramps. Here we are and somehow the gun got back in the bag. I don't know how or why, but I'm sure there must be some explanation."

"I'm sure there is." Gramps said staring into the fire.

"May I see the revolver?"

"Sure Gramps," I said handing the old gun to him. "Do you have any ideas of what's going on?"

Gramps ignored my question. He held the revolver by the firelight and turned it over a couple of times. He then looked over at Scooter and asked, "What did you mean when you said this old gun feels like a hundred dollar bill?"

"Oh!" said Skinny. "I almost forgot! My Great Uncle just came to town yesterday and said he'd give a hundred dollar reward to anyone providing proof of what happened to the lost boy."

"Why would he want to do that?" Gramps asked.

I didn't know if I should have been giving out any information or not, but I couldn't help myself. "Because," I began hesitatingly, "Scooter's uncle, Henry, said he was the lost boy's brother and he wants to find his remains and give them a proper burial."

"What!" Gramps cried, handing the revolver back to me. "Henry, the lost boy's brother? Are you sure?"

"That's what he said," Scooter answered. "Don't ask me. I've only known him one day. He lives out in California and I've only heard my mom talk about him once in a while."

"How old is your uncle?" Gramps asked.

"I don't know. I suppose in his sixties or seventies."

"Why did he wait until now?" Gramps asked.

"He didn't," I said, defending Henry. "He said that he came back when he was a young man and searched for a while, but never found anything, and then he had to go back to California."

Gramps never said a word. He slowly stood up and walked around the fire. I could tell something was bothering him. He then sat back down on the log and stared into the flames with misty eyes. Slowly his head dropped down into his hands and his shoulders began to shake softly.

Scooter looked at me with a frown and silently mouthed a question. "Is he crying?"

"I think so," I mouthed back, glancing between Scooter and Gramps.

Scooter and I sat there in awkward silence, not sure of what to say or do. Finally I got up and walked over to Gramps, placing my hand on his shoulder. "Gramps? Is something wrong?"

Gramps raised his head with a smile. Big tears slowly ran down his cheeks. I didn't know what to do.

I had never seen a grown man cry before, especially an old grown man.

"What is it Gramps?" I asked.

Gramps reached in his back pocket, took out a faded red handkerchief, wiped his tears and blew his nose. Putting the handkerchief back in his pocket, he turned to us and said, "I'm sorry boys, but you really caught me off guard."

"What do you mean Gramps?" I asked.

Gramps stared into the fire for a few moments and then, with a big sigh, began to explain. "Since you boys have revealed your secrets to me, I guess it's only fair that

I reveal mine to you, Lord knows I've carried them for too many years."

Scooter and I looked at each other questioningly. "Secrets?" I asked, "What secrets?"

"Well," Gramps began, "To begin with, there is no ghost of Ghost Lake."

"Huh?" I said, "No ghost? How do you know?"

"Well, it's kind of hard to explain, but I'll give it a try."

"Did you know the lost boy?" Scooter asked.

"Sort of," Gramps said with a smile.

No wonder Gramps was acting so strange! I knew that he hadn't told us the whole story! I began to put two and two together and I was sure the answer was four. I was really enjoying playing detective and I thought I had the case solved.

"Gramps," I began. "You are the one who put the revolver back in the tent bag aren't you?"

"Yup," said Gramps. "You're right about that. I've been watching you boys off and on all night. I overheard that Barnswell kid talking to another kid about how he was going to scare you boys tonight, so I figured maybe I'd come up and warn you. I arrived about the time you were digging up the grease can, so I just stood back in the shadows and watched."

"So, you're the one that Blanca was barking at!" Scooter exclaimed.

"Yes, the first time," Gramps admitted. "But then I gave her a couple of treats and we have been good friends ever since."

"What about the other times?" Scooter asked.

"The other time, after the rainstorm, it was the Barnswell kid. I had seen where you boys had put the revolver in the tent bag and I figured maybe that kid would steal it. So, I sneaked into your camp and took the gun."

"And you returned it just now when you came back and lit the fire." I said, still trying to play detective.

"Yes, I knew how much it must have meant to you boys to find the revolver and besides, I just wanted to look it over and hold it for a while. It's been about sixty years since I've held that old revolver."

"You buried the revolver in the grease can?" Scooter asked.

"Yup, I was the one, you see… you're sitting right here by the fire with the lost boy of Ghost Lake."

You could have knocked us both over with a feather!

STORY TOLD

❖ ❖ ❖

Gramps had really dropped a bombshell on us! What a mystery! I could hardly believe it. We were actually sitting here with the legendary lost boy of Ghost Lake.

"Wow!" Scooter exclaimed. "Then Uncle Henry really is your brother?"

"Yup, and I can hardly wait to see him. You can't imagine how many years it's been."

"I'm sorry Gramps," I said, "But I don't understand. Why have you kept this a secret all these years?"

"It's a long story, but let me start at the beginning."

Scooter and I both had goose bumps as we squirmed closer together on the tent bag, anxiously waiting for Gramps to go on. Gramps walked over and placed a few more sticks on the fire. He then asked if he could see the revolver again. I handed it to him and he sat back down on the log. He turned the revolver over a few times and then holding in the flat of his hands he stared into the fire and began his story.

"This Colt .44 belonged to my father, Earl Frankson, town marshal of Deadwood, South Dakota in 1889. People say he was the best marshal that Deadwood had ever had. He was well liked and fair, but firm. Law and order was the rule of the day."

"Gosh!" I whispered, looking at the old revolver in a new light. "He was a real marshal! What happened to him?"

"Like I said, he kept law and order. One day in May of '89, three outlaws rode into town and tried to hold up the town bank. My Pa didn't have a deputy, so he had to take on the outlaws alone. They came out of the bank shooting and Pa was waiting for them. He gunned down two of them on the bank steps, but the third one made it to his horse where he grabbed his rifle and shot my Pa in the back. Pa fell bleeding in the dusty street of Deadwood, but with his dying breath he managed to raise this old Colt and drop the last outlaw."

Scooter and I were speechless for a few moments. What we had heard was something you saw in a movie or read in a book. It didn't seem possible that we were hearing this first hand from the marshal's son and that we had actually found the revolver that had gunned down three outlaws in 1889.

"Were you old enough to remember it, Gramps?" I asked.

"Oh yes," Gramps said. "I was only eight years old, but I can still remember that terrible day. My brother Henry was only a tiny baby, so I don't imagine he'd remember any of it."

"What did your mother do?" Scooter asked.

"Well, it was like life had ended for her also. She was left a widow with no means of support and two little kids. She'd gotten a five hundred dollar reward for the outlaws, so she packed up us kids and boarded a stagecoach for back east where she had some relatives. She kept Pa's gun, marshal's badge, spurs, and gold watch. She wanted us kids to have these to remember our Pa. I still have the gold watch." he said, pulling out an old gold watch and snapping it open to show us.

In the inside cover of the watch was a picture of a pretty young woman and a little kid. "Is that your mother and you?" I asked.

"No," Gramps said with a sigh. "That's another story, but anyway, my mother brought us two boys back east to a little town called Lewiston, about fifty miles from here."

"Is that where you grew up then?" Scooter asked.

"No, we were just passing through when my ma saw a sign for help wanted in a boarding house, so she hired on and worked there for a year or so."

"What's a boarding house?" I asked.

"Oh, it's like a hotel where they rent rooms to workers and they get there meals there also. Ma cooked in the kitchen and cleaned rooms on the weekends."

"I see," I said. "Then what happened?"

"Well, after a year or so, my ma met and married a fellow by the name of Josh Quade. He had homesteaded some land over here by Ghost Lake and he moved us all back here. After we were here about a year and a half, ma took sick with the flu and passed away, leaving me and Henry with Josh Quade."

"Boy! That must have been rough on you kids!" Scooter exclaimed.

"It wasn't too bad at first, but I missed my ma something terrible. Then Josh Quade remarried about a year later and that woman was a mean one. She wasn't too bad with little Henry, as he was only a couple of years old, but she sure made life miserable for me! Then Quade took to drinking and everything went sour. He'd come home drunk, get in a fight with his wife and end up beating me around. I took it all that winter, but made up my mind to run away that summer, as soon as I'd turn thirteen."

"How did you decide on which day to go?" I asked.

"Well, a few weeks before I ran, I stashed away some beans, bacon, and other grub in the woods over here. As far as picking the day, I guess Josh Quade picked it for me. One night in July he came home drunk and slapped me up and threw me around the house. That night I made up my mind to run, so just before daylight I packed up my pa's things, left a note that I was going berry picking, sneaked out the back door and disappeared."

"Was it hard to go?" Scooter asked.

"The hardest part was leaving little Henry. I had grown really fond of the little jigger, and after all, he was my only real living relative that I knew of. I can still remember the morning I left like it was yesterday. I tip-toed over to his crib, lifted him up and hugged and kissed him. I promised him and myself that I'd come back and get him in a few years and take him with me, but that didn't work out either."

Gramps paused for a moment with a lump in his throat and tears in his eyes. It was an awkward moment, but I didn't blame him. I was on the verge of tears myself and looking over at Scooter, I could see he wasn't in any better shape.

I tried to get Gramps mind off of little Henry and the painful separation.

"What happened to the marshal's badge and your pa's spurs?" I asked.

A hint of a smile returned to Gramp's face. "Well," he began, "I believe if you were to dig around in that there grease can, you'd probably find them down near the bottom."

Scooter and I dove for the grease can at the same time and began scooping out big handfuls of grease. Within two scoops I came across the star shaped marshal's badge and three scoops later, Scooter came up with the spurs, tied together with a short length of baling wire.

"Wow!" exclaimed Scooter. "Where are those rags? Let's get these cleaned up!"

Moments later, the badge and spurs shined, almost grease-free, in the palms of our hands. "Gee Gramps," I said. "For a while there, I couldn't believe that you could have been the lost boy, but these prove beyond a doubt that you were the only person that could have possibly known that they were in the can with the revolver."

HISTORY REVEALED
❖ ❖ ❖

We sat back down by the fire and inspected our new found treasures. We then handed them over to Gramps and he looked them over. He smoothed out one of the cleaner rags and placed the revolver, the marshal's badge, and the spurs together. Stepping back, he looked down at them, and then turned his misty eyes up to the stars and whispered. "Here they are Pa. We're all together again."

Scooter took a deep breath and let out a big sigh. Getting up from our tent bag, he walked over to the little woodpile and brought back a few sticks, adding them to the fire. It was a special moment that none of us wanted to break by speaking. We sat in silence by the gun, the badge, and the spurs, almost feeling that another ghost was present, that of Gramp's dad, the fallen town marshal. In handling the articles, I felt like I had known him myself, like I had dreamed about him or something. It was weird, but I could picture what he looked like and what Deadwood must have looked like in 1889. I finally shook it off as my imagination and decided to pursue my line of questioning.

I broke up a small twig and threw it into the fire, breaking the silence. "What happened after you ran away, Gramps?"

Gramps, picked up where he had left off. "Well, as I told you before, I had packed a little grub off into the woods over here. I figured they'd come looking for me, so I packed everything up and hiked down to the other end of Ghost Lake. I decided to stay there for a while until I could decide what I wanted to do."

"It wasn't called Ghost Lake back then, was it Gramps?" Scooter asked.

"No...Some people called it Turtle Lake, but most people just called it the lake. Anyway, I managed to hide from the search party for a few days and then by the end of the first week, they had pretty much given up. After about ten days I had the woods to myself and I must say I managed pretty well until my grub ran out. It was nip and tuck for a while and I even thought about going back home. In fact, one night I did sneak back to the house. I crawled right up to the kitchen window and peeked in."

"Nobody even knew you were there?" I asked.

"Nah, I had gotten pretty good at sneaking around, and anyway, old man Quade was drunk as usual, so he wouldn't have heard me. I remember I sneaked up on the porch and slithered along the wall until I came to the open window. I just stuck around long enough to hear the old man swear that if he ever did find me, he'd beat me senseless. I decided right then and there to make plans the next day to clear out of the country."

"What did you do for food?" Scooter asked.

"Oh, I managed to raid a few hen houses," Gramps said smiling, "And then berries were in season and I'd go along the lake and catch a few bullfrogs and crayfish and cook them up in a frying pan I had stolen. I was getting to the point where I was getting pretty good at surviving."

"You ate bullfrogs? Yuk!" Scooter exclaimed. "What can you eat on a bullfrog?"

"I'll tell you what," Gramps said, "You boys go out and catch a mess of bullfrogs one of these days and I'll cook up the batch for us. You just use the back legs and I guarantee you'll like them better than chicken."

"No thanks," Scooter said. "Why didn't you use the revolver and shoot some rabbits or something like that?"

"Well, I didn't want to make any noise and tip anyone off that I was still around, and besides, I was getting along fine the way it was. I didn't really need to use the gun."

"Why did you bury the revolver Gramps?" I asked. "And where did you get the grease?"

"That came about sort of by accident. After a few weeks, I got kind of brave and became careless in my wandering about. I was down at the other end of the lake, in one of the back bays, hunting for frogs and crayfish, when I came around a little point of bull rushes and right there in front of me were two men fishing from a small boat. They spotted me about the same time I saw them and I quickly jumped back in the woods and disappeared. I could hear them hollering and calling to me, but I just kept going. I knew right then that I'd have to leave or there'd be another search party looking for me."

"And they thought you were a ghost!" Scooter added.

"I guess so," Gramps said, "But anyway, I knew I'd have to leave, so that night I sneaked into town and stole this here can of grease from the blacksmith shop. I had already picked up a hatchet and a shovel, so it was just a matter of packing the revolver, spurs, and badge in the grease can and burying it."

"Why didn't you take them with you?" Scooter asked.

"Yeah," I chimed in, "And why didn't you mark the spot where you'd buried them?"

Gramps looked up at the sky. "It'll be daylight soon. Aren't you boys getting tired?"

"No!" We said in chorus. "Finish your story!"

Gramps smiled and picked up the revolver. "I thought about taking them with me, but then, how would it have looked for a thirteen year old boy to be wandering around the country with a revolver and a badge and spurs? As far as marking the spot, I did. I buried the grease can exactly half way between two big pines that grew up on this little hill. I knew the grease would keep everything from getting rusty, and anyway, I was planning on coming back in a few years."

"What went wrong?" I asked.

"A lot of things, "Gramps murmured, "I traveled further and stayed away longer than I had planned was the main reason. I bummed my way to the Mississippi where I got a job on a riverboat and spent my teenage years between New Orleans and St. Louis. I finally wandered back here when I was almost a grown man and nobody recognized me. I had changed my name and grew a beard and in no time had fit right in."

"Why did you change your name and where was your family when you came back?" Scooter asked.

Gramps looked up at the sky, getting lighter by the minute. "It'll be daylight soon and I'll be danged if you boys don't have a lot of questions. But...I guess we've got a few hours yet before I can see Henry, so I reckon I can finish the story for you."

"Good deal!" I exclaimed, getting up to throw more wood on the fire.

"My real name was John Frankson, and I figured that the law might be looking for me as a runaway, so I just turned it around and called myself Frank Johnson. When I came back to town I snooped around and found out the Quades had moved out the summer after I disappeared and nobody had seen or heard of them since. I then went looking for this grease can and found out that these woods had been logged over and then a forest fire had gone through. I had no idea where to look as everything looked the same. I tried for a couple of days, but it was a lost cause."

"So, you settled down and have lived here ever since?" I asked, trying to guess the end of the story.

"Yes," Gramps sighed, "Except for while I was in the army, I've been here ever since."

"Did you ever get married?" Scooter asked.

"Yes I did, but not for a long time after I had returned to Ghost Lake."

"How old were you then?" I asked.

"Well...let's see..." Gramps said thinking out loud. "I was married in 1915...so I guess I was in my early thirties."

"What did you do for a living and what happened to your wife?" Scooter asked.

"Hold on a minute!" Gramps said in exasperation. "You boys ask more questions than a couple of newspaper reporters."

I gave Scooter a poke with my elbow, indicating to him that his questions were getting kind of personal, but Gramps didn't seem to mind talking about it.

By this time the sun had begun to peek through the trees and the woods came alive with the chirping of birds. Gramps poked up the fire and sat down to finish his story.

"I learned the telegraph trade soon after I returned to Ghost Lake and I went to work for the railroad, sending and receiving messages. I worked there for a number of years and then met and married a young lady that came to work at the depot."

Gramps hesitated for a few moments and poked at the fire with one of our hot dog sticks. I could tell it was painful for him to be remembering all of this, but he wanted to continue.

"About a year later, we had a little girl and she was the prettiest little thing you ever saw. Two years later we had another baby on the way and World War I broke out. I didn't think I'd have to go, as I was over thirty, but the army wanted me for my telegraph skills and called me up. I didn't want to leave my wife with a little toddler and another on the way, but they didn't give me any choice. Before I knew it, I was through basic training and headed for France. They sent me right up to the front where I was sending and receiving war messages. I wasn't there a month when the Germans launched a big offensive and over ran our position. I was pretty shot up in both legs and the Germans captured me. They sent me to a prisoner of war hospital deep in Germany and the army reported me missing in action and presumed dead."

"Wow!" I exclaimed, "How long were you gone?"

"I suppose it must have been a year or so since I had had any contact with home and when I did get home, everyone was surprised. They all thought I was dead, and I wished that I was when I got back here."

"Why was that Gramps?" Scooter asked.

"Oh, it was a real mess. My wife had passed away giving birth to our second daughter and they had no way of notifying me, in fact, they thought I was dead too. So, they took the baby and adopted her out to another family and sent my other little girl out west somewhere to live with some relative of my wife's. I spent the next couple of years looking for the girl's, but it was like they had disappeared off the face of the earth."

"So...you never found them?" I asked.

"No, I tried off and on over the years, but always came up empty handed. I even put ads in newspapers and magazines, but nobody ever answered them."

Poor Gramps, he had lost his mom and dad, Henry, his wife, and two little girls. I couldn't imagine so much sorrow heaped up on one old man. I picked up the old Colt revolver and looked up at Gramps, trying to cheer him up. "Well Gramps, it looks like you've found Henry anyway."

"Yes, thank God for that," Gramps said with a smile as he looked at the sun climbing up over the trees. "C'mon, I'll help you break camp and then we'll go down to my place and get some breakfast. I'd like to clean up and shave before I go to meet my baby brother."

In twenty minutes we had packed up our gear, doused the fire, and headed down the trail. For the first time in fifty some years, the revolver, the spurs, and the marshal's star were in the hands of their rightful owner.

CLEANING UP

❖ ❖ ❖

We stepped out into the bright sunshine on Ghost Lake Road. This was going to be a special day.

I could just feel it. I wondered what the reaction was going to be when Henry and Gramps were reunited. Along with last night, this was more excitement than I'd had for three years. Gramps surprised us again as we started up the road.

"I suppose you boys would like your rake and shovel back."

"You took them?" Scooter asked.

"No, but I saw where that Barnswell kid hid them. He thought he was pretty sneaky, but I was watching him all along."

"Why that dirty rat!" I exclaimed. "Where did he hide them, Gramps?"

Gramps pointed up the road about fifty feet. "There's a culvert there that runs under the road. He put them in there."

"Speak of the devil," Scooter said pointing up the road. Coming around a curve, far down the road, was Arnold, riding his bike. Scooter looked at his watch. "Five minutes to seven, right on time."

Arnold came riding up and jumped off his bike. "Well, if it isn't the happy campers!" he sneered. "Looks like you had to have a baby sitter along."

"I don't see your comic books Arnold." I said for lack of anything better to say.

He laughed. "No, and you're not going to see them either. You never said anything about bringing Gramps along. That doesn't count as spending the night alone in the woods."

Scooter bristled at Arnold's remarks. "Listen, for your information we did spend the night alone. Gramps just came up to our camp this morning."

"Yeah? Well, I guess you'll just have to prove it."

At this point Gramps entered the conversation. "Hold it son, they're telling the truth and where I come from, a man's word is taken seriously. I was a witness and I say they spent the night alone in the woods."

Arnold should have kept his mouth shut, but then he never did learn respect. He had to make the situation worse. "Hey, just because you're an old man, doesn't make me believe it any more."

It was Gramps turn to bristle. "No? Well, I happen to know another old man, Grandpa Barnswell, who is as honest as the day is long, and I'm sure he'd believe me. He'd also appreciate hearing what a brat his grandson is. Now, perhaps you'd like to reconsider what you're doing."

Gramps had hit Arnold's soft spot. The thing most kids feared most. The possibility of their folks or their grandparents finding out that they had done something they shouldn't have. I almost felt sorry for Arnold, as he knew he would have to eat some crow and didn't like the idea of it.

"Well...uh...if...if you say that they were in the woods all night...then I guess I'll have to take your word for it. I'll bring the comics over this evening."

"I'll tell you what, Arnold," I said, trying to make peace and be honest about the whole affair. "Gramps did come up to our camp pretty early, but we did spend most of the night alone. Why don't we just call it a draw and forget about the comics."

Arnold seemed satisfied with this arrangement as it gave him a chance to save face and also fifty comics. "Well, I guess that would be fair. I can agree to that."

"Oh...and Arnold?" I said, deciding not to let him off the hook completely. "One other condition."

"What's that?" he asked.

"We'd like our rake and shovel returned."

"What? How'd you know?"

"Never mind," I said, "We'll just wait here while you get them."

"Oh, all right," he said, walking over to the culvert.

In a short time he had returned with the missing tools. I thanked him for returning them and he rode off grumbling under his breath.

"Well Gramps," Scooter said. "It looks like you came through for us again. I'm beginning to think you're some kind of good luck charm."

"Yeah Gramps," I chimed in. "Thanks for the help. Now, what's the plan for the rest of the morning?"

Gramps looked us over from head to toe. I took a good look at Scooter and saw what Gramps was looking at.

Scooter's uncombed hair stuck out in four directions and his face carried the evidence of last night's ordeal. Traces of dirt from our digging blended with touches of grease from the can. Smoke and charcoal smudges from the fire outlined the faint line of dried marshmallow around his lips. His shirt and jeans were no better. Traces of everything were smeared on his clothing from head to toe and besides that, he had slept in them.

Glancing down at myself, I concluded that I must look pretty much the same. I looked up at Gramps and asked, "Pretty bad, hey Gramps?"

Gramps smiled and shook his head. "You two look worse than I did after running wild for two weeks. I'd say we'd all better get cleaned up before we do anything. C'mon, let's go to my place."

A short time later Gramps was frying bacon and eggs while Scooter and I scrubbed our face and hands and dug clean clothes out of the packsack. We were drying our faces on the towels Gramps had provided when he called from the kitchen.

"Come and get it boys!"

Scooter and I attacked the bacon, eggs, and toast like a couple of wolves. I hadn't realized how hungry I was until I began eating. "Gee, this is great, Gramps!" I mumbled with a mouthful of food."

"I'm glad you like it." Gramps answered. "You boys go ahead and finish up. I'm going to go take a quick bath and get slicked up a little before I go to meet Henry."

Scooter and I finished eating, rinsed the dishes in the sink, and then refilled the kitchen sink and washed our faces and hands again and combed our hair. We then went into the living room to wait for Gramps.

"Have you known Gramps long?" Scooter asked as he sat down on the sofa.

"All my life," I answered, picking out the big easy chair to sit in. "My mom's always taken a liking to him and we've had him over lots of times for Christmas, birthdays and special occasions. I guess she felt sorry for him being all alone and wanted to include him in our family."

"Yeah, I know what you mean," Scooter said. "I never had a grandpa. My dad's father died when I was a baby and I don't think my mom even knew her dad."

"Well," I said. "We've kind of adopted Gramps as our honorary Grandpa and that's the way I think of him."

"He's really a neat old man," Scooter said, deep in thought. "I wish I could adopt him as my grandpa."

"Well Scooter, I'm sure we could share him. I mean, it's not like we got him through an adoption agency or anything."

"Yeah?" said Scooter, perking up. "I'd like that."

As the conversation lulled I looked around the room. "Look, here are some pictures on the wall."

Scooter and I walked over and looked at the pictures Gramps had hanging. "This must have been Gramps in his army uniform," I said, pointing to a picture of a young man in a faded photo.

"And this must be him and his wife," Scooter said pointing to a young couple with a little girl.

"Boy, she sure was pretty," I commented.

"Yeah, what a shame," Scooter added.

We heard Gramps stirring in the back room and we scooted back to our chairs. We didn't want him to think we were snooping. I hissed to Scooter and pointing at the pictures, put my finger to my lips, indicating not to say anything about the pictures. I didn't want to break Gramp's good mood now that he was about to meet Henry.

Gramps walked into the living room looking like he was going to church. "Well, it looks like you boys cleaned up some also," he said opening his arms, "How do I look?"

"You look great Gramps. "Shall we go?"

"Randy," Gramps said, pausing to think, "Why don't we call your mom and ask her to come with us? She's always been kind of special to me and I'd like her to be with us when I meet Henry. I think she'd be proud of the part you played also."

"Good idea Gramps. I think she'd like that, but we won't let the cat out of the bag until you meet Henry."

"Yes, let's keep it a surprise until then." Gramps said.

I called mom and told her we were safely out of the woods and at Gramps' house. I then told her that Scooter's mom would like to meet her and that Gramps was going to walk over with us. Mom agreed that she would be ready when we stopped by in about twenty minutes.

"Are you going to take the gun, badge, and spurs, Gramps?" Scooter asked.

"I suppose we should," Gramps said, "Just in case Henry doesn't believe our story."

Gramps put the revolver in a brown paper bag and tucked the badge and spurs in his shirt pocket. Stepping in front of a long mirror in his hallway, he gave himself a once over to make sure he was presentable. "Well...here goes nothing," he said taking a deep breath. I could tell he was really nervous and I can't say that I could blame him.

Fifteen minutes later we arrived at my house and mom immediately wanted to know all about our camping trip and if we got rained on. We played our story down and told her we had a good time and nothing unusual had happened. We didn't want to spoil Gramps' surprise.

As we approached Scooter's house, Gramps became visibly nervous. "Uh...boys...Hold it a minute. Uh...could I talk to you in private for a minute?"

"Sure Gramps," I said. "Mom, could you excuse us for a minute?"

We walked up the sidewalk about twenty feet, leaving mom with a curious frown on her forehead.

"What's up Gramps?" I asked.

"Well, this is going to be kind of awkward. I haven't seen Henry in over fifty years and I'm not sure where to begin."

"I've been thinking about that," Scooter said with a sly grin, "And I think I have a workable plan."

We put our heads together and listened to Scooter's plan. In about one minute he outlined what seemed to be a great plan. It was amazing how he seemed to come up with these ideas, and they always seemed to have a dramatic flair to them. This was going to be fun to watch!

Mom waited patiently as we walked back to join her. I could tell that she suspected us of being up to something, but wasn't sure if it was good or bad.

"I'm not sure what you three are up to," she said with a little smile, "But it had better not include me."

"Don't worry mom," I assured her. "It's not bad or anything."

"All right," she said, "But if you embarrass me in front of Scooter's mother, I'll ground you for a week!"

Scooter and I giggled and Gramps chuckled to himself as we walked up the sidewalk to Scooter's house.

THE REUNION
❖ ❖ ❖

Scooter's mom stepped out the door as we walked up the front sidewalk. A look of worry and concern told us that she felt something was wrong. She had never met Gramps or my mom, and I imagine seeing Scooter and me with these two adults, she assumed we were in some kind of trouble. Parents always seem to think the worst when they don't know what's happening.

"Good morning," she said hesitantly. "Is everything all right? Are you boys in some kind of trouble?"

"Morning mom!" Scooter said, running up and giving her a big kiss and a hug. "Nothing is wrong; I just brought some people over for you to meet. You know Randy, and this is his mom."

My mom shook her hand. "Hello, my name is Aimee. Scooter is certainly a nice boy and Randy and he get along very well."

Scooter's mom returned the greeting. "It's nice to meet you, Aimee, I'm Carrie. I'm glad Scooter has found such a nice friend so soon after arriving here."

Scooter broke into the conversation, "And this is Gramps. He's a special friend of Randy's and he helped us out last night. I wanted him to meet Uncle Henry."

"That would be nice," Scooter's mom said. "Won't you come in for a cup of coffee?"

"Thank you," Gramps and my mom said as they walked up the steps and into Scooter's house.

We walked into the living room and Gramps set the paper bag containing the revolver down by his chair. I caught Scooter's eye and mouthed the question, "Where's Henry?"

Scooter shrugged his shoulders to indicate he didn't know.

Again I mouthed a statement, "Ask your mom."

Scooter turned to his mom, "Where's Uncle Henry, mom?"

"He's upstairs shaving. Did you want to see him?"

"Yeah," Scooter answered, "I'd like to introduce him to Gramps and Mrs. Bigsley."

"Why don't you go up and get him, Scooter." She said. "I'll go and put on a fresh pot of coffee."

Scooter started up the steps, but stopped on the first landing, waiting for his mom to start the coffee. He wanted to make sure everyone was in the living room before he brought Uncle Henry down for this historic reunion. In a few minutes Scooter's mom came out of the kitchen and he scooted up the steps to fetch Uncle Henry.

I had butterflies in my stomach, anticipating the meeting of the long lost brothers. I could imagine how Gramps must have felt. I noticed he was sitting with his hands folded, fingers nervously dancing while his feet did a slow shuffle under his chair. I couldn't imagine remembering back fifty years. I couldn't remember what happened ten years ago.

A slight cough at the top of the stairs warned us that Scooter was about to make his grand entrance. He purposely came slowly down the stairway to increase the drama of this event. I glanced over at Gramps and for a moment thought he was going to blow Scooter's plan. His eyes grew misty as he saw Henry, but he held his composure and stood up as Scooter led Henry into the living room.

Scooter led Uncle Henry to the center of the room for the introductions. "Uncle Henry, I'd like you to meet some friends of mine. This is Randy's mother, Mrs. Bigsley, and this is a friend of ours, Gramps Johnson."

They all shook hands and exchanged greetings, although I thought Gramps showed a little too much enthusiasm in shaking Henry's hand.

Scooter's mom brought in the coffee and a plate of cookies. Everyone exchanged small talk about the weather and how fast the summer had gone by. My mom started talking about her garden and was offering everyone tomatoes and cucumbers. I squirmed on my chair, thinking the subject was never going to get around to the reason we were here. I finally caught Scooter's eye and nodded toward Henry.

He got the message and skillfully turned the conversation in the direction we wanted. "By the way, Uncle Henry, have you had any luck in your search?"

"No Scooter," he answered. "In fact, the few people I've talked to look at me like I'm crazy. Most people have never heard of the legend and the ones that have don't believe it. There are only a few old timers around who were here at the time, but most of them were too young to remember what had happened."

Knowing my mom, I could have predicted that she couldn't keep her curiosity in check. "What exactly are you searching for, Henry?" she asked, then added, "That is, if you don't mind me asking."

Aha! She had fallen perfectly into Scooter's trap! He knew that if he raised the question, someone would pick up on it and get Uncle Henry to tell his side of the story.

"Well ma'am, it's a long story," he began. "I was only a young pup myself when it all took place, so I don't know the details, but I'll tell you what I know and what I'm looking for."

He went on to relate how his older brother had gone off picking berries, disappeared, and was never to be found. He then told of how the legend grew and of the sighting of the boy, known as the Ghost of Ghost Lake and of how the lake and the community came to be named after the incident.

"It's bothered me for many years that my brother never had a decent burial and that is the reason I'm here now, to find his remains and give him a final resting place."

"How sad!" my mom commented. "I know the feeling... I lost my parents when I was a baby and I've always wondered what they were really like."

"Yes, it's a sad world," Uncle Henry agreed. "Things don't always work out the way we'd like them to."

All this time Gramps sat there listening, remembering, and not saying a word. I felt that he wanted to jump in and tell who he was, but wasn't sure of how to do it.

My mom, a natural talker, picked up the slack in the conversation and kept it rolling in the right direction. "My goodness!" she exclaimed. "I grew up in Brewster, a little town about forty miles from here, and even there we heard stories of the ghost of Ghost Lake. I always thought they were just stories, but to think that they were true, and to even meet the brother of the lost boy is more than I can imagine!"

"Well," Henry continued, "I don't know if there actually ever was a ghost...you know how stories are sometimes. I can tell you for a fact, that there was a lost boy and that he was never seen again."

Scooter chose this moment to put phase two of his master plan into play. "Uncle Henry," he began, "The newspaper article said something about the lost boy having a gun with him. Do you know anything about that?"

"Yes," Henry said, "Many years later I found a diary in the belongings of my stepfather and stepmother. It was a diary kept by my real mother. I suppose they had meant to give it to me in later years, but apparently had forgotten all about it."

With this new information, Gramps could hardly contain himself. "A diary?" he asked. "Belonging to your real mother?"

Henry did not notice the sudden interest by Gramps. "Yes," he went on, "And in the diary she told of my real father, Earl Frankson. He was the town marshal of Deadwood, South Dakota and was killed in a gunfight with some outlaws. Mother packed up my brother and me and headed back east. Apparently the revolver they mention in the article belonged to my father."

"Do you remember seeing the revolver, Uncle Henry?" I asked.

"I imagine I probably did see it, but I was so young, I can't remember it. My mother's diary also mentioned that she had kept his marshals star and spurs, but I suspect that my stepfather probably sold them to buy liquor."

Enter phase three of Scooter's plan. With a dramatic flair, Scooter walked over to Gramp's chair, picked up the paper bag, and walked back over to where Uncle Henry was sitting. Keeping the bag closed, he began a speech I'm sure he had been rehearsing in his head for the past twenty minutes.

"Uncle Henry," he began. "I know how important this search is to you and I know that you have offered a hundred dollar reward for information about your brother..."

Pausing for a moment, Scooter motioned for me to join him at the table.

Remembering our secret conversation on the sidewalk, my mom became suspicious of what we were doing. "What are you boys up to?" she asked.

"You'll see, Mom," I said. "Wait a minute please, and let Scooter finish."

Scooter continued. "As I was saying...first of all, I think that Randy and I can help you...and we won't take the hundred dollar reward either."

That was nice of Scooter to say that, but I thought the least he could have done was consult with me before giving up my half of the reward.

"In fact," Scooter said smiling, "I think you had better hang on to your hat when you hear the story we have to tell."

"What do you mean?" Uncle Henry said, also wondering what we were up to.

"Well...," said Scooter, putting his hand down into the bag, "When Randy and I were camping. We dug a fire pit at our campsite...and accidentally discovered this!"

With the finish of his sentence, he withdrew the revolver from the bag and placed it in front of Uncle Henry.

It would have been fun to have dropped a pin at that time. I would have been willing to bet the hundred dollar reward that you could have heard it easily.

For a few moments everyone's eyes shifted from the revolver to each other and then back to the revolver. Uncle Henry then slowly reached for the revolver while Gramps sat silently in his chair, a knowing smile on his face.

"What do you mean? You accidentally found this revolver?" Uncle Henry asked. "How did this happen?"

Thus began phase four of Scooter's plan. It was his moment of glory...his day in the sun. Uncle Henry examined the revolver while Scooter took a deep breath and began telling our story. I have to give him credit. He told the story with just the right amount of humor and suspense, skillfully building the suspense to the part when we unearthed the can and the revolver. Here he stopped for a moment, leaving out the part about Gramps, the marshal's star, and the spurs.

All the while Scooter was telling his story, Uncle Henry was listening intently and checking over the old revolver. When Scooter stopped for a moment, Henry placed the old revolver on the table and exclaimed, "This is it! This is my father's Colt revolver. Look here!"

Everyone leaned forward and looked at our treasure. "See these initials carved on the handle!" Henry said excitedly. "E.F.!...Those are my father's initials...Earl Frankson!"

"So...it must have been placed there by your brother." My mother said quietly.

"Yes, it would have had to have been my brother...it couldn't have been anyone else!"

Scooter's mom asked, "What do you think happened?"

Uncle Henry thought about this for a moment. "I...don't know...but, I'd be willing to bet that his remains can't be too far from where you boys found the revolver. I'll change my clothes and we'll get a couple of shovels and go back to the campsite."

"Not necessary, Uncle Henry," Scooter said importantly.

Uncle Henry raised his bushy eyebrows. "What do you mean...not necessary?"

"Because...," Scooter said, pausing for effect, "What would you say if we told you...we have already found the remains?"

Uncle Henry's jaw dropped. Scooter's mom jumped out of her chair, a little angry. "Leonard Dobson! You had better stop playing games and tell us what you have to tell us and I mean...now!"

Even at that, Scooter maintained his composure and dramatically placed phase five of his master plan into effect.

He slowly walked across the room, turned and placed one hand on Gramp's shoulder. When all questioning eyes were on him he extended his right palm forward and said, "Uncle Henry...I would like you to meet your brother...John Frankson...the lost boy of Ghost Lake."

For sure you could have heard a pin drop now!

BROTHERS AND SISTERS
❖ ❖ ❖

Uncle Henry sat there speechless! Mom's hand flew up to cover her mouth in shock. Both moms' eyes darted back and forth, from Gramps to Henry, to each other, and back to Gramps and Henry. Gramp's eyes misted up again as I went over and stood by his side. Scooter came over with an ear to ear grin and we shook hands with the realization that this was the greatest moment that had happened for either of us. For us, it was the happiest of endings in which we took the total credit for solving the mystery of the lost boy of Ghost Lake.

Gramps finally broke the silence. Getting up from his chair, he walked over to Uncle Henry and placed the marshal's star and spurs in front of him. Putting his hand on Henry's shoulder, he said, "Its true Henry...I've kept this secret for long enough."

Tears rolled down both of their cheeks as the long lost brothers hugged each other. Our moms came forth with handkerchiefs and sniffed and snuffled with teary eyes. I have to admit, it was a moving moment and I confess also, that I had a huge lump in my throat and more than a few tears escaped my eyes. Looking over at Scooter, I could see he was having the same problem as me.

After a few moments, everyone regained their composure and began asking questions at once.

Gramps held up his hand, "Hold it! Hold it!" Silence fell over the room. Gramps continued, "I think it would be easier if Henry and I took turns telling our sides of the story. I'm sure it would answer a lot of questions for everyone."

"Wait!" Scooter's mom said, suddenly producing a camera. "I'd like to take some pictures first." Twisting big plastic flashbulbs into her camera, she snapped pictures of Gramps and Henry, Scooter and me with them, and the four of us holding the revolver, badge and spurs.

"I guess that'll do for now," she said, putting the camera down. "O.K. Gramps, let's hear your story."

Gramps sat back down in the easy chair and began his story. He began with the early years out west and then of how his mother brought him and Henry back east. It was pretty much the same story he had told Scooter and me at the campsite. When Gramps came to the part where he had decided to run away, he turned and apologized to Henry.

"I'm sorry I left you Henry, but I couldn't take living in that house for one more day. I wanted to take you with me, but I was only thirteen and had no means of taking care of you."

"I never blamed you," Henry said. "I had always been told that you had gotten lost in the woods and had never been found. I always believed that story until I got a little older and was better able to think things over. At one time I even figured maybe Pa Quade might have done you in and buried you back in the woods someplace. Thank the good Lord I was wrong."

Gramps shook his head. "It must have been tough for you growing up in the same house with that man."

Henry said, "No, it wasn't as bad as you might think. Of course, I can't remember much about the early years, in fact, I can hardly remember moving out to California."

Scooter piped up, "Was old man Quade as mean to you as he was to Gramps?"

"Not really," Henry said. "When we got out to California, he got a job on a fishing boat and would be gone to sea for weeks at a time, so I didn't see a whole lot of him. The boat would come back to port to sell their fish, maybe stay a weekend or so, and then go out for another two weeks or so."

"What about your stepmother?" I asked. "How did she treat you when you were home alone with her?"

"Well," Henry said, "We had a neighbor woman that got her involved in religion and turned her right around. She was never mean to me after that, but I sure spent a powerful lot of time in church and Sunday school. She even persuaded the old man to give up drinking and that helped the living conditions also. Things went along pretty good until the big storm of 1907."

"What happened then?" I hurriedly asked.

"Well, I believe it was in April of '07, a beautiful spring day, and Pa Quade's fishing boat put out to sea with nary a sign of bad weather. By that evening the sky clouded over and the wind began to build. All that night the wind screeched and howled and rain came down by the trainload."

"Was it a hurricane?" Scooter asked.

"I don't know as I've ever seen a hurricane, but if this wasn't one, I'm sure it was the next thing to it. Anyway, after three days the storm calmed down some and the wreckage of Pa Quade's fishing boat was washed up on the beach. An effort was made to find survivors but nobody saw hide nor hair of any of the crew again."

"How old were you then, Henry?" My mom asked.

"I was fifteen or so. I was old enough to go out and get a job anyway. I found work as a stock boy in a grocery store and I worked there for a number of years. Other than that job, the only means of support we had was a little washing and ironing that my mother took in. She had had rheumatic fever when she was a young girl and in effected her in later years. Her heart finally gave out and she passed away when I was in my early twenties."

"What did you do then?" I asked.

"Well, I didn't have any brothers or sisters, so I had to take care of their affairs and settle the estate. When I went through all the papers I found out that Pa Quade had kept his original property back here in Ghost Lake. I was still a young man and had no ties, so I figured I'd come back here and try my hand at farming. It was at this time also that I found the diary that had been kept by my real mother, Carissa Frankson."

"Do you still have the diary?" Gramps asked.

"Yes, I rented a safety deposit box at a bank out west and I put the diary in there, along with my other important papers."

"I'd sure like to read it sometime," Gramps said.

"And you shall, John, or should I call you Frank? I imagine you're used to being called Frank after all these years."

"That's a fact," Gramps agreed. "But it's also good to hear my real name after all these years."

"Well I've always thought of you as my brother John, so if you don't mind, I'll call you that."

"Fair enough," Gramps said, and then added. "What year did you come back here to farm, Henry?"

"Let's see," Henry said, pausing to think. "After my step-mother died I tried a few different jobs for awhile. Then I tried joining the army when the war broke out, but they wouldn't take me because of my bad eyes. It would have been about that time. I'd say about the spring of 1918."

"That explains why I never heard of you or saw you," Gramps said. "That was about the same time I was drafted into the army and shipped to France."

"Why didn't you stay here, Uncle Henry?" Scooter asked.

"Hmmph! I guess I found out the same thing Pa Quade did years before. You can't grow good crops in sand and rocks. And then I had met my wife and she had taken Carrie to raise, so I didn't see any future on the farm with a family to support. We talked it over and figured that California had a lot more to offer, so we packed up and moved back west."

"What line of work did you get into out there?" Gramps asked.

"The real estate business," Uncle Henry said. "California was beginning to boom back then and property was selling like hot cakes."

"What about you, John?" Scooter's mom asked. "What happened to you after you ran away?"

"It's a long story," Gramps said with a sigh. Leaning back in his chair, he retold the story of his youth on the

Mississippi and of how he later returned to Ghost Lake and met and married his wife. He mentioned his little girl and of how he was drafted, sent off to war, captured and held prisoner while everyone thought he was dead.

"Uh...What happened to your wife?" Scooter's mom said with a strange look on her face.

"When I finally was released from the prison camp I made my way back here to Ghost Lake only to find out that my wife had died in childbirth with our second daughter. I was told my little girl had been taken by some relatives, but nobody seemed to know who or where they had taken her."

"Did the baby survive?" Henry asked.

"As far as I know," Gramps said. "They told me at the hospital that she was premature and was kept in the hospital for many months until she was well enough to survive and then was adopted out to another family. I tried for years, off and on again, to find some trace of either girl, but I never had any luck. I finally gave up and I've been a bachelor ever since."

"Why Gramps," my mom said. "I never knew that."

Scooter's mom sat down silently, her face as white as a ghost. "What...What was your wife's name?" she stammered.

"Rose," Gramps said quietly. "Rose Marie. I used to sing the old song to her...Oh Rose Marie, I love you, and I'm always..."

Dreaming of you," Scooter's mom finished the line. "Of all the girls I've ever known, I love you, my Rose, my Rose Marie."

Gramps smiled. "You know the song too? It was our favorite. We'd sit out on the back porch in the evening and I'd strum on an old guitar and sing that song to her." A tear glistened in his eye as he recalled those times of long ago.

"And your little girl, Carissa, named after your mother, would sit by your chair and play with a rag doll named Toody," Scooter's mother whispered.

"How do...you?" Gramps began, but couldn't finish.

"Oh daddy!" Scooter' mom cried as she ran over to Gramp's chair and threw her arms around him. "I remember, I remember!"

The rest of us sat in shock, trying to sort out in our minds, what was happening here. My head was spinning with visions of Gramps, Henry, little girls and ghosts. How did this happen to be?

"I was only three..." Scooter's mom said, softly crying. "But those are my earliest memories...the back porch, the guitar, and my rag doll, Toody. I still find myself humming that song at times when I'm in an especially good mood. Oh! I can't believe this is happening!"

Gramps hadn't said a word. He just hugged and hugged Scooter's mom. I didn't think he was ever going to let her go, but finally he released her and held her at arms length. "My little girl," he finally managed to say. "My darling little girl."

Henry, coming out of shock, finally managed a few words, "I had no idea. We always called her Carrie. I didn't make the connection that it was short for Carissa. Why didn't I realize it?"

Gramps reached into his watch pocket and brought forth the big watch we had seen at the campsite. "I have a picture of you and your mother," he said opening the watch.

Scooter's mom held the watch gently for a few moments and studied the picture of her and her mom. "She was beautiful, wasn't she?" she said, passing the watch to Henry.

"Yes, she was," Henry added, passing the watch around the table for the rest of us to see.

Scooter and I looked at the picture. You could see the resemblance between his mom and the lady in the picture.

There was no doubt that this was her mother. "Here mom," I said passing the watch over to my mother.

Taking the watch, she studied the picture for only a moment when her eyes widened and her hand rose up to cover her opened mouth. "Oh! oh!" she cried as she stared at the picture.

"What's the matter mom?" I asked.

"Are you ill?" Henry said.

Mom shook her head vigorously, "I...I...," she said, unable to continue.

"What is it, Aimee?" Gramps said walking over to her chair and putting his arm around her shoulder.

Mom couldn't say a word. Tears rolled down her cheeks as she raised her arms and unfastened a chain from her neck. She withdrew the chain with a silver locket at the end and placed it on the table. All eyes were on her as she opened it with trembling fingers. With the locket open, she placed it in the center of the table for all to see.

A gasp rose from all of us! There in the locket was the very same picture that Gramps had in his watch! Confusion flooded over me as I tried to understand the significance of this.

"Where did you get this?" Henry asked.

"My adopted mother gave it to me on my twelfth birthday," my mom finally managed to utter. "She said it was the only thing they had sent with me as a tiny baby coming from the hospital. She guessed it was my real mother, but had no idea who she was or what had happened to her. In those days, adoption agencies did not tell anyone of the history of babies they gave out."

Gramps, with a look of shock, picked up the locket and whispered, "I sent this locket to Rose from France. It was about two days before I was wounded and captured."

Silently my mom stood up and threw her arms around Gramps. He closed his eyes and squeezed her tightly, then motioned for Scooter's mom to join them. The three of them hugged and kissed each other, weeping happily at their joyful reunion.

I couldn't believe what was happening. What were the odds that something like this could be true? But, it was all there, the proof of the entire story. The revolver, badge, and spurs, the matching pictures, the remembered song. It had to be true! This meant that Gramps really was my Grandpa, and Scooter's too! I laughed to myself at the realization of what all of this meant.

I winked at Scooter and motioned for him to join me outside. Standing out on the back porch, I shook his hand and put my arm around his shoulder, "C'mon cousin, let's go for a walk."

AND THEN...
❖ ❖ ❖

Randy closed his notebook and put his pen down. That was it. The end. It made for a pretty good story, he thought. Maybe some people might not even believe it, but then, he couldn't quite believe it himself.

His mom and Aunt Carrie had been inseparable since the discovery and the two of them had been over to Gramp's house just about every day, cooking, cleaning and visiting. Of course, they had a lot to catch up on. Uncle Henry had gone back to California. He said he was going to sell his property and move back to Ghost Lake to be close to Gramps and his two nieces.

And then there is Scooter. Things haven't changed much between them. Even though they found out they were cousins, they still consider each other the best of friends. Right now Scooter is worried about school starting and how he's going to get along. He knows it'll be a lot easier having Randy for a friend, but its still a nervous experience for someone new to a school. You miss your old school and your friends for awhile, but then before you know it, you're one of the gang and having a good time.

Arnold hasn't been hanging around much. It probably bothers him that he didn't come out on the winning end of the deal and doesn't want his friends to find out that he isn't as cool as he thinks he is, but he's the kind of kid who'll forget in awhile and come up with some kind of dirty trick. That's half the fun of it, trying to outwit Arnold and his gang of friends.

Randy smiled as he thought about what had happened. It was going to be fun to write it all down. In fact, he thought to himself, I'm going to write different stories about this coming school year and I think I'll call it "The Ghost Lake Chronicles."

Author's note: This book, The Legend, is the first in a series of Ghost Lake Chronicles books I have planned. All characters are fictional, based on childhood memories of mine, for I too, was twelve years old in 1952. I have tried to bring a flavor of what it was like for a young boy growing up at that time. If you enjoyed the book and would like to send me a comment, I would very much like to hear from you. Send an email comment to: ghostlakechron@hotmail.com